THE SECRET
OF DEVIL MOUNTAIN

The ambassador has vanished, limousine and all.

But Supergranny is on the trail through the rugged West Virginia mountains.

It's the wildest adventure yet for the senior sleuth with the red Ferrari, the Poindexter kids, Shackleford and Chesterton, the world's most spoiled robot.

Should they trust mysterious, long-lost cousin Boots Bowen? Is Old Jellie a friend, a foe or just a common, ordinary black bear? And what secret hides deep in the shadows of Devil Mountain?

Supergranny Mysteries

Supergranny 1: The Mystery of the Shrunken Heads
ISBN 0-916761-10-X
Library Hardcover: ISBN 0-916761-11-8

Supergranny 2: The Case of The Riverboat Riverbelle
ISBN 0-916761-08-8
Library Hardcover: ISBN 0-916761-09-6

Supergranny 3: The Ghost of Heidelberg Castle
ISBN 0-916761-06-1
Library Hardcover: ISBN 0-916761-07-X

Supergranny 4: The Secret of Devil Mountain
ISBN 0-916761-04-5
Library Hardcover: ISBN 0-916761-05-3

Supergranny 5: The Character Who Came to Life
ISBN 0-916761-12-6
Library Hardcover: ISBN 0-916761-13-4

Buy Supergranny mysteries at your local bookstore, or ask the bookstore to order them. Or order them yourself with this coupon.

Holderby & Bierce, Publishing
P.O. Box 4296
Rock Island, IL 61201-4296

Please send the Supergranny mysteries checked above. Enclosed is my check or money order for $_____ ($2.95 for each paperback, $7.95 for each hardcover; plus $1.50 postage and handling per order.)

Name _____

Address _____

City _____ State _____ Zip _____

Allow 2 weeks for delivery.
Prices subject to change and offer to withdrawal without notice.

SUPERGRANNY

THE SECRET
OF DEVIL MOUNTAIN

To Heather —

Happy Adventures!

Beverly Van Hook

Beverly Hennen Van Hook

3/30/94

Holderby & Bierce

Published by Holderby & Bierce, P.O. Box 4296,
Rock Island, IL 61201-4296

Andrea Nelken, editor

Paperback. ISBN: 0-916761-04-5
Library Hardcover. ISBN 0-916761-05-3

SUMMARY: Supergranny and friends set out to help a long-lost relative in the Appalachian Mountains of West Virginia and become entangled in international intrigue involving a missing ambassador. Senior citizens on a bus tour help the Supergranny gang crack the case. Fourth in the series about a gray-haired detective who drives a red Ferrari and fights crime.

Holderby & Bierce, October, 1988
2nd Printing December, 1989

Printed in the U.S.A.

To Mary Alice and Johnny
and to my beloved West Virginia
on its 125th birthday.

1

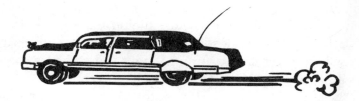

The black stretch limousine ran us right off the road.

One second there we were, hiking happily along, enjoying the mountain view. The next we were diving for the ditch.

Whoosh, the limo with little flags flying from its windows rounded the curve, whipped past and disappeared around the mountain.

Whoosh, a dark gray Ford followed it.

Whoosh, whoosh, whoosh, whoosh, whoosh, a chain of dark gray Fords whipped by and disappeared like a snake around the curve.

"Stay put, there might be more," Supergranny warned. Supergranny's real name, as you may already know, is Sadie Geraldine Oglepop, and she lives next door to us in Illinois.

I'll explain in a minute what we were all doing in the West Virginia mountains, but first back to the limo and chain of Fords.

Whoosh, sure enough, here came another Ford.

Whoosh, whoosh, here came two more.

The dust settled and the mountain road became very still.

"I think that's the last of them," Supergranny said, pulling her mini-robot, Chesterton, from under a tree root where he'd gotten stuck while hiding from the limo.

Chesterton is battleship gray with buttons and dials all over him. He's smart, funny, about the size of a loaf of bread, and, I'm sorry to say, spoiled rotten.

"WELL," huffed my older sister, Angela, dragging our Old English sheepdog, Shackleford, back onto the road. "SOME people think JUST BECAUSE they drive a stupid LIMO they have the right to run decent citizens RIGHT OFF THE ROAD."

"Joshua, go look behind us to see if anything else is coming," Supergranny said to me, "while I check out Vannie."

My younger sister, Vannie, had landed in a blackberry bush and picked up a few scratches. Supergranny wanted to be sure she was OK. She was. I could have told Supergranny that. Vannie specializes in falling into blackberry bushes or off horses or worse. It doesn't pay to get excited about it.

Anyway, I inched back along the road, hugging the mountainside, and peered out at the hairpin curve we'd just climbed. You could see the road winding down the steep mountain valley for at least a mile. It was as quiet as church.

"All clear," I said. "Unless they turn around and try to get us again."

I was joking, of course. I knew the drivers of the limo and chain of Fords weren't really after us.

Not then.

Unfortunately, that was going to change.

*   *   *   *   *   *

We were on our way to the rock cliff Mom had told us about for years.

It was just up the road from Boots Bowen's house. Boots is Mom's favorite cousin. He'd called long distance two days before because he was in some kind of trouble and needed help.

He'd really called for Mom. He didn't know she and Dad were in Spain celebrating their fifteenth wedding anniversary. Supergranny and Chesterton were staying with us while they were away.

It had been a strange call, and Mom seemed upset about it when she and Dad called us from Madrid that night.

"Well, what kind of trouble did he say it was?" she kept asking.

"He didn't say," Angela kept answering. "He just said he needed a little help and wanted to talk to you and Dad."

"That's just not like Boots," Mom said again. "He's so darned independent. How did he sound?"

"He sounded fuzzy," Vannie said. "The line was bad."

"That's just not like Boots," Mom said again. "He's always doing for others. I can't imagine what the trouble

3

is. How did you say he sounded?"

"Fuzzy," Vannie said.

The next thing we knew, Mom was ready to turn around and come home.

So what if it was her first trip to Spain?

So what is it was her and Dad's fifteenth wedding anniversary?

So what if she didn't get another vacation from the newspaper for a year?

Boots was her favorite cousin and we knew he'd loaned her money to study journalism at Marshall University. She'd only told us about it 135 times.

We also knew she'd been half mad at him for years for the way he took off after graduating from Harvard and traveled around the world and hardly ever wrote to let anybody know where the heck he was and spent a lot of time as a beachcomber in Buenos Aires and who knows where all.

But he was still her favorite cousin.

He was still the one who loaned her the money to study journalism at Marshall University.

"You call Boots back and tell him we're coming home," she said. "Tell him we'll be there in 48 hours."

That didn't suit Dad and Supergranny.

They got on the line and decided the Illinois contingent would visit Boots. (That's what Dad called us, "the Illinois contingent"; he and Mom were "the Spanish contingent.")

Two minutes later Supergranny was on the phone to Boots, telling him we were driving out to help.

"What did he say?" Vannie asked when she hung up.

"He said, 'All right, now if I'm not there you all make

yourselves at home. The key is hooked under the rocking-chair seat on the front porch.' "

"At least, I think that's what he said," she added slowly. "The line was fuzzy."

We left the next morning, stayed overnight in Kentucky, and had just arrived in the West Virginia mountains.

Boots' little house was empty, but we figured he'd be back soon. We found the key, unloaded the Ferrari, then hiked up the road to the rock cliff to stretch our legs.

The rock cliff path Mom had told us about was just around the curve where the limo had disappeared. It was overgrown, but we were able to find the footholds and climb up and onto the bare, rounded sandstone overlooking waves of mountaintops.

"Look, the limo!" Angela said, pointing.

Sure enough, deep in the dark green valley, the limo had turned off the road and stopped.

"Look at that," Vannie said. "The bushes are parting."

Supergranny whipped her binoculars out of her purse, took a quick look and passed them around.

Vannie was right. The bushes parted and raised like an arch. The limo, followed by the chain of Fords, passed under the arch and into the woods.

It was dark in the mountains, and there was still no sign of Boots.

"We'll give him one more hour, then I'm calling the sheriff," Supergranny said, looking up from the "USA Today" she was reading.

We'd come back from the rock cliff, unpacked, and picked about 38 million wildflowers to put in jars in Boots' kitchen.

By then we were pretty hungry, so Supergranny rummaged around and found some beans and salad, then pulled out cornmeal, eggs and stuff to make cornbread.

"We'll just fix ourselves a nice little supper on Boots," Supergranny said. "He DID say to make ourselves at home."

Now Vannie and I were playing dominoes by lamplight

on the kitchen table and Angela was reading an old "Five Little Peppers" book with tan pages she'd found in the bookcase. A kid had written her name in it in brown ink — "Gwinn Bowen." The kid was Mom.

Ten more minutes passed.

Angela put down the Peppers and glanced at the black pendulum clock on the mantle. It looked like a little house with a steep roof and had a painted glass picture of a bunch of people around a fireplace. They were all dressed like George and Martha Washington.

"Where the heck do you think he is?" Angela asked. "This is starting to feel a little odd."

"Odd?" I asked. "Walking into a stranger's empty house, fixing cornbread and beans, then sitting down to play dominoes? You call that odd?"

Vannie laughed. "Goldilocks did it. Sort of."

"What do you mean, 'stranger'?" Supergranny asked. "You mean you've never actually met Boots? I thought he was one of your mother's dearest relatives."

"Well, yes, when they were kids," Angela said. "But before we were born he graduated from Harvard and took off around the world."

"And we lived in Ohio," I said. "Then we moved to Illinois."

"But he did send us pictures," Vannie put in. "He sent us a picture of himself on the beach when he sent me that doll from Argentina."

About then we heard the shots. Except we didn't know they were shots. It was a loud cracking. Like blasting. Or a car backfiring. Or fireworks. Or shots.

Whatever it was, it woke up Shackleford. She jumped

7

up, paced around, then went over to the kitchen and stared out into the evening. She kept making little whimpering sounds and her ears twitched.

That woke up Chesterton, who switched on his lights and beeper and sprang from the kitchen table to the refrigerator for a better look out the window.

Then Shackleford barked and we heard crashing outside the back door.

"BOOTS!" Angela yelled, dashing to open the door.

"DON'T TOUCH THAT DOOR — !" Supergranny yelled.

Angela froze.

" — yet," Supergranny said more calmly. "Sorry to startle you, dear. Let's take a look out the window first."

We gathered around the window and peered into the shadows. At least we gathered as well as we could around a jumping, barking, agitated Old English sheepdog.

More crashes. And there on the back porch was the crasher himself, nosing around the porch floor for stuff he'd just knocked out of the garbage can. He looked as big as a snowmobile and his dark fur glistened in the lamplight from the window.

"Oh, look! Cute! Adorable!" yelled Vannie, becoming more agitated than Shackleford. "A little black bear."

I don't know where she got "little." There wasn't anything little about him.

"What if he decides to come in?" I asked Supergranny nervously.

"He'll come right in," Supergranny said. "And we'll go right out the front, understand? Automatically. I don't want anybody standing around arguing with him." She laughed.

"But he won't decide to come in."

I don't think she was so sure herself, though, because she scooped Chesterton off the refrigerator just in case we had to make a getaway.

With Vannie yelling, Shackleford barking, the bear crashing, and Chesterton beeping and whirring and trying to hop out of Supergranny's arms for a better bear view, nobody heard the front door open behind us.

"Well, look who's here," a voice boomed.

We whirled around to see a huge, red-bearded man striding across the kitchen.

"BOOTS!" we yelled.

"Just like the picture you sent with my doll from Buenos Aires," Vannie said.

"Quick, close the front door," Angela said. "There's a bear out there."

Boots laughed and hugged us. "That's Old Jellie. He won't bother us . . . but I am a little worried about the folks shooting at me back up the road."

Sometimes it's tough knowing what to say when you meet a long-lost relative.

Not this time.

Gunfire down the road and a bear crashing around on the back porch broke the ice.

"Is it dangerous?" Angela asked. "The bear, I mean."

"Is he friendly?" Vannie asked. "Old Jellie, I mean. Can I pet him? Is he yours, Boots?"

"Who's shooting at you?" I asked. "And why? And are they still shooting? Did they follow you here? Should we call the police? The sheriff?"

"How are your folks?" Boots asked. "What are they doing in Spain? Is that a robot? How was your trip? Is that a Ferrari outside? Did you have any trouble finding the key? Isn't that kind of small for a robot? Whose Ferrari is it? Have you eaten?" Boots asked.

"Would you like some of your beans?" Supergranny asked.

Meanwhile, Shackleford raced around the kitchen in circles and Chesterton, who never misses a chance to go totally hyper, hopped out of Supergranny's arms and back on top of the refrigerator, whirring and beeping and blinking like a police helicopter convention.

The kitchen was totally out of control.

Supergranny whipped her whistle out of her apron pocket and blew.

It was piercing. Tornado sirens whisper compared to Supergranny seriously hitting the whistle.

Even Old Jellie stopped crashing around on the porch. The shots stopped, too, although I didn't notice it at the time because my ears were ringing from the blasted whistle. Boots was thunderstruck. I guess he'd never seen a gray-haired woman in a blue polka-dot dress and stars-and-stripes tennis shoes blowing a whistle in his kitchen before.

If that surprised him, I'd like to see him duck through her fireplace into her secret office-workshop-laboratory-playroom-garage . . . but more about that later.

Anyway, everything stopped but the pendulum clock.

Supergranny smiled, nice as pie.

"Now, Angela, dear, maybe Boots would like you to warm up these leftover beans," she said sweetly.

Boots nodded that he would. He was still thunderstruck.

"Joshua, fix Boots a nice cup of tea," she said.

11

"Vannie, set Boots a place and get out the rest of the cornbread and salad."

"Shackleford, lie down in the corner and stay there."

"Chesterton, GET DOWN OFF THAT REFRIGERATOR."

Everybody did as told, and I could see Old Jellie slinking off into the woods as I filled the teakettle.

If Boots minded her taking over his kitchen, he was too polite to say so. Or too scared.

He just grinned and sat down at the place Vannie set for him. Supergranny pulled the rocker near him, leaned back and propped her feet on a three-legged footstool. As soon as the beans were warm, Angela loaded up his plate and we all sat down around the kitchen table.

Shackleford dozed in the corner.

Chesterton flipped off his lights and beeper and slid down the refrigerator and under the table.

The clock ticked.

"To answer your questions, Boots, yes, Chesterton has been my robot for years, and I guess he is rather small, although I've seen smaller," Supergranny said. "I'd like to apologize for his behavior tonight. Sometimes he gets a little overly excited."

Angela, Vannie and I coughed. "Overly excited," she called it. The most bonkers-prone robot in civilization and she called him "overly excited."

She shot us a quick look.

We stopped coughing.

"And, yes, that's my Ferrari we drove from Illinois," she continued. "You're welcome to take it for a spin tomorrow if you'd like."

Boots grinned. He'd like it, all right. Who wouldn't?

"And now, as soon as you've cleared up a couple of questions about Old Jellie, let's get down to business," Supergranny went on.

"What's this mysterious 'trouble'?"

Boots shoveled in the beans and looked thoughtful.

He slathered apple butter on the cornbread and looked thoughtful.

He stared at his tea.

"It's hard to know where to begin," he said.

"How about with Old Jellie?" Vannie prompted.

He laughed. "Well, Old Jellie lives in the state park just the other side of Devil Anse Mountain."

"Devil Anse?" Angela butted in. "Is it named for Devil Anse Hatfield? As in the Hatfield and McCoy feud?"

Boots nodded. "But we usually call it Devil Mountain for short." The rest of us groaned. We groaned because we knew what was coming. Angela's next sentence would begin, "I did a report —"

"I did a report on the Hatfields and McCoys, and —" she said.

"AGGGHHHHHHGH," Vannie said and slid off her chair under the table.

Angela, as you may know, has done a report on almost every subject in the world and has gotten at least an A – on every one of them.

Unfortunately, she's never forgotten one word or comma in any of them and I predict she never will. Worse, once she starts to talk about a report, you CANNOT — repeat — CANNOT shut her up.

Except this time. This one historic occasion.

13

"Tomorrow, Angela," Supergranny said firmly. "You can give us a blow-by-blow report of the complete fifty-year Hatfield and McCoy feud TOMORROW. But we've driven 600 miles to help Boots and we start TONIGHT. No detours."

"OK, OK, OK," Angela said.

I couldn't believe it. I thought she must be coming down with the flu. Or maybe she just wanted to find out if Old Jellie was a people eater. Whatever the reason, she pretended to zip her mouth, lock it and toss the key over her shoulder.

"You were saying Old Jellie lives on the other side of the mountain," Vannie said, scooting back onto her chair.

"Yes, you may have noticed a little yellow tag on his ear," Boots said.

(Not me. I was too busy noticing how to get out the front door if Jellie came in the back.)

"Several families of black bears live in the park, and the rangers tag them and try to protect them. But old Jellie has been spoiled by tourists feeding him. They mean well, but it's bad for Jellie and bad for us."

"Why?" Vannie asked.

"Well, because Old Jellie doesn't know where the park stops or when bear season starts. If he steps outside that park and lumbers up to a hunter to beg for peanuts in bear season — it's 'Goodbye, Old Jellie.'"

"That's awful," Vannie said. "Poor old thing, thinking someone's going to give him peanuts and getting shot instead."

"Yeah, and it would have been more awful if one of you kids had accidentally surprised him on the back porch."

14

"You mean he might have attacked?" Angela asked.

Boots shrugged. "Who knows what a wild animal will do if it thinks it's cornered?"

"This makes me feel much better," I said sarcastically.

Boots laughed. "Just be sensible, and Old Jellie won't bother you. I'll show you a better place to put the garbage from now on. Don't go outside without a flashlight at night. Make enough noise to let him know you're coming."

"Like Mom yelling, 'Snake! Snake!' " Vannie said.

Boots looked at her blankly.

"When she used to visit here," Vannie said. "When she went through the weeds to the swinging bridge, she'd always yell 'Snake! Snake!' so they'd know she was coming and skedaddle . . . don't you remember?"

"Oh, sure. I forgot," Boots said.

"Moving on," Supergranny said. "About this 'trouble'?"

Boots stared at his tea again.

He sighed, hunched over the table and cradled the teacup in his hands.

"How much did I tell you on the phone about Ambassador Haji Jamad?"

4

"Who?" Angela asked.

"Haji What?" Vannie asked.

"You didn't tell us anything as far as I remember," I said.

"Well," Boots said. "It's not important, actually this trouble thing is probably overblown, it's not really —"

"Haji," Supergranny broke in. "It seems to me I do remember something . . ." she said slowly. "Oh, yes, Haji Jamad, Balkhastani ambassador.

"Balkhastan. Tiny country near Afghanistan," she went on, gaining speed. "Mountainous. World's largest producer of lapis lazuli, a beautiful blue semi-precious stone. Jamad's making an official visit to the U.S. this week. An old friend of yours, isn't he, Boots?"

Angela, Vannie and I stared in amazement.

When in tarnation had Boots told her all that? I was right beside the phone when she talked to him. I didn't remember anything about Jamad.

I tried to ask her but she motioned me to be quiet.

"Let Boots finish his story, Joshua. Let's not interrupt."

It was some story.

"Haji and I were college roommates at Harvard. He was a little guy, just 5'7" or so, and brilliant.

"At first he didn't say much about Balkhastan; he was more interested in hearing about West Virginia.

"And I was sure glad to talk, because I was homesick," Boots said with a laugh. "I went on and on about our long, lazy springtime, about whole canyons of wild rhododendron in bloom, our wonderful storytellers.

"He was interested in everything. From how we broke off from Virginia to stick with the Union during the Civil War to the problems of mountain road building.

"Since he came from mountainous country, too, he could joke about farming on an angle. We told the Bostonians up at Harvard that we planted potatoes on top of the hill and at harvest time dug holes in the bottom to let the potatoes roll out."

"That's a slick system," Vannie said. "Does it really work?"

Boots laughed. "We were just kidding them, Vannie. But we had those Bostonians half believing us."

"Finally, Haji began to talk about Balkhastan," he went on, "and I found out he was crown prince."

"A real prince?" Vannie asked.

"As in royal blood?" Angela asked.

17

"I don't know anything about royal blood," Boots answered. "But there *was* a royal battle. Haji's pop beat out his cousin, the old king, in battle. The cousins and the different tribes were always getting mad and sweeping across the mountains to fight one another in those days. They had a new king every twenty minutes or so.

"Haji's father was made king in a giant ceremony complete with elephant races, fireworks and tribesmen dashing around on camels, waving spears and singing.

"Haji was just seven at the time, but he remembered it like it had happened last Tuesday.

" 'Wonderful ceremony, Buuts,' he'd say. He always pronounced 'Boots' as 'Buuts.'

"Anyway, it was a glorious ceremony and fitting, too, because the elephants and camels weren't just decoration. Oh, no. They were USED. When it came to roads, Balkhastan didn't have squat, so people got around on camels. They'd have camel caravans five miles long.

"And they used the elephants to drag the cannons up the mountains for war.

" 'Doesn't that tek the cek, Buuts,' Haji would say. He'd heard me say 'that takes the cake' once, and after that he was forever saying 'that teks the cek.' He spoke seven languages, and gave English slang his own original twist.

"Anyway, he was teed off at his father and the older generation for wasting so much time and energy dragging cannons up mountains by elephant.

"He thought they should be building roads and dams and training doctors to save babies instead.

" 'Half our babies die, Buuts,' he'd say, getting very upset. 'Half die because we don't have doctors. Doesn't that tek the cek?'

" 'Shhhtupid,' he'd say, shaking his head. He meant it was stupid to let half your country's babies die while you piddled around dragging cannons up hills with elephants. 'Shhhtupid, shhhtupid, shhhtupid.'

"He made me promise I'd come to Balkhastan when he became king and help him modernize.

"I sort of promised without realizing it, just sort of drifted into promising.

"Next thing I knew, we'd graduated. Haji went home and I came down here. The very next week I heard on the radio that Haji's dad had been assassinated and Haji and his family had been chased into a mountain hideout near the Kasbad Pass.

"Then I got the envelope. The envelope that took me away from home. It started those wandering years when I sent you that picture from Brazil, Vannie.

"There were three things in it:

"— A one-way ticket to New Delhi, India,

"— The name of a tribal guide in New Delhi who'd take me to Balkhastan through the Kasbad Pass,

"— A note with two words . . . 'Hurry, Buuts!' "

5

Boots stayed in Jamad's mountain stronghold for six years. Together with the help of about 100 soldiers and their families, they turned that primitive mountain camp into a modern democratic state. Refugees from other parts of Balkhastan swarmed in to help.

Finally, the people in the rest of Balkhastan rebelled against the dictator who had killed Haji's father. They threw him out and invited Haji to return to the capital as their first elected president.

He went.

He wanted Boots to come, too, but Boots figured he'd done his part for Balkhastan. And he'd had enough.

"I wanted to see the rest of the world," Boots said. "Well, I saw it. I got so tired of traveling I felt like Mark Twain

— that if I ever got home I hoped someone would shoot me in both legs so I wouldn't travel again.

"I just got back to West Virginia last year.

"Meanwhile, old Haji served two terms as president, then was secretary of state and I don't know what all. Last year he was named roving ambassador.

"Two weeks ago, he sent me a secret cable that he would be coming to the United States on official business. He's meeting someone from the U.S. State Department at the elegant Greenbrier Hotel in White Sulphur Springs tomorrow and he wants me there — secretly. Under cover.

"NO ONE was supposed to know about that cable." Boots' voice trailed off. "And that's when the trouble started," he said softly.

"Someone broke into the cabin while I was in town and turned the place topsy-turvy. Only one thing was missing: Haji's cable.

"Then the phone calls started. 'Stay away from Jamad,' a husky voice would warn. I'd get calls two or three times a night, sometimes at midnight, sometimes 2 or 3 a.m.

"And finally, the shots. Three different ambushes, counting tonight. Pzzzzing, pzzzzing, pzzzzing, right across the hood of the pickup."

"And why did you call Mom?" Angela asked.

"I had to talk to someone I could trust," Boots answered. "I couldn't sleep because of the durned phone threats and I was getting so jumpy I couldn't think straight. I had to talk to someone.

"I've been away so much, my old friends are scattered. But I knew I could trust your mom no matter what happened. It wouldn't matter if I hadn't seen her in a hundred years.

21

"I thought if she and your dad could meet me we could go over all this. Help me get a handle on it. Help me figure out what to do.

"And that's how it stands.

"Someone knows I leave at noon tomorrow to meet Haji Jamad secretly at the Greenbrier Hotel.

"And someone's out to stop me."

*   *   *   *   *   *

That night Supergranny, Angela and Vannie bunked in the spare bedroom and I got the couch.

It was on the lumpy side, and I had a hard time sleeping.

Every time I'd forget about the lumps and drift off, I'd dream I heard Old Jellie bursting through the back door or gunshots bouncing off the Ferrari outside the window. Then I'd wake up again.

I made up for it the next morning, sleeping so late that everyone was gone when I woke up. I had cornbread and juice, then found Angela out back, sitting on the swinging bridge eating half a tomato.

It was fresh out of Boots' garden and was as big as a grapefruit. She handed me the other half.

It was the best tomato I'd ever eaten.

"Where's Boots?" I asked.

"Town," Angela said, staring into the creek and slowly chewing tomato. "Took the Ferrari."

"Where's everybody else?"

"Picking blackberries," she said, still staring at the creek, looking lost in thought.

"Shackleford and Chesterton, too?" I asked.

She didn't answer. She just stared at the creek.

I tried again. "Shackleford and Chesterton, too?"

"Yep," she said slowly. "And Vannie's Walkman." Vannie had a new Walkman and she wore it almost everywhere.

Silence.

Obviously, to use one of her favorite Words of the Week, something was on Angela's mind. She was forever landing on some mildly fancy word like "obviously" and using it to death, then dropping it to move on to something fancier.

Whatever was bothering her, sooner or later she'd tell me.

And frankly, I wasn't in any hurry to hear it.

It was a hot, sunny, lazy morning and it was nice to sit on the swinging bridge, watching dragonflies dart around down by the water.

The weeds seemed to be humming with a million crickets. Except they weren't crickets, Supergranny had told us the day before. They were cicadas. They made the weeds seem so alive. I liked the sound.

After our 600-mile drive, being run off the road by a stretch limo and chain of Fords, being terrorized by a black bear and gunshots, and sleeping (and not sleeping) on the world's lumpiest sofa, it was nice to sit on a peaceful old swinging bridge in the sunshine, eating a tomato and listening to the weeds.

Too peaceful. I knew it wouldn't last.

It didn't.

"Something's wrong," Angela said.

"Well, sure," I said. "Someone's trying to break up Boots and Haji's secret meeting. Sure, something's wrong. That's not news."

"No, I mean Boots. Something's wrong about Boots." She stopped staring at the creek and stared at me instead. She looked sad.

"Didn't you notice anything?" She asked.

She was making me feel very uncomfortable. There HAD seemed something wrong in the back of my head. I mean WAY back. Behind the room where my actual thinking goes on.

"I like him," I said.

"But didn't you feel something wasn't quite right last night?" she asked.

I wished she would let well enough alone. I wished some little brain buzzer wouldn't keep agreeing, "Something's wrong about Boots. Something's wrong about Boots."

I nodded. "I felt it, but I hoped I was wrong. What bothered you?"

"Several things," she said. "All small. But when added together. . . ." She lapsed into creek-staring again.

Now that she'd brought it up and wrecked the whole peaceful morning, I wished she'd get on with it.

"What?" I said. "Whatwhatwhat???"

"Number One," she said, "he wasn't going to tell us about Haji at all until Supergranny indicated he'd already mentioned him on the phone." ("Indicated" was another past Word of the Week.)

"Number Two, he didn't remember Mom saying 'Snake, snake' when she walked through the weeds.

"Number Three, when he first came in, Vannie said he

24

looked just like the picture he'd sent her from Buenos Aires. Later he referred to the picture he'd sent from Brazil."

"So?" I asked.

"Wake up, Joshua. Buenos Aires is in Argentina. It *isn't* in Brazil."

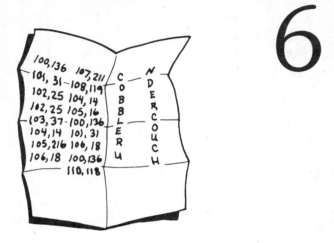

6

"Oh come off it, Angela," I said. "That was probably a slip of the tongue. Besides, lots of people mix up Argentina and Brazil."

"Really?" she asked sarcastically.

"Adults?

"World-traveling adults?

"World-traveling adults who send their nieces dolls from there?"

"Well, sure," I said lamely. "Anybody can make a mistake."

Angela sort of sniffed. *She* would never mix up Argentina and Brazil. Or Tuscaloosa, Alabama, and Turkey, Texas, either, for that matter.

"Never mind," she said. "The main thing is, I think Supergranny smells a rat, but doesn't want to tell us."

26

"What do you mean, 'smells a rat'?" I asked.

"I mean she suspects something is wrong about Boots," Angela said. "Rewind your mind to last night. Remember when Boots asked how much he'd told us on the phone about Haji?"

I nodded.

"And when none of us could think of anything, he said it wasn't important and tried to change the subject?"

I nodded again.

"Until Supergranny broke in with all that stuff about Haji and Balkhastan. The lapis lazuli mines and all that?"

"Yeah, when did they talk about all that on the phone?" I asked. "I was right there, I —"

"They didn't. Read this," Angela said.

She tossed me yesterday's "USA Today," which she'd been reading. "USA Yesterday," I guess you'd call it.

The story was in the "Statesline" section, which has one paragraph of news from each state:

WEST VIRGINIA
WHITE SULPHUR SPRINGS —
Undersecretary of State Anthony Elliott arrived at the Greenbrier Resort Hotel today in preparation for official meetings with roving ambassador Haji Jamad of Balkhastan, a tiny, mountainous democracy near Afghanistan. Jamad, former president of Balkhastan, the world's leading producer of lapis lazuli, has strong ties to West Virginia, which he visited often while an undergraduate student at Harvard.

27

I whistled. "So that's where she got that stuff. But why did she tell Boots they'd talked about all that on the phone — that he'd just forgotten?"

"She didn't SAY it; she IMPLIED it. To get him to tell us about the trouble."

I whistled again. What was going on? Why was Supergranny trying to trick Mom's favorite cousin?

We both stared at the creek some more.

Finally, Angela grabbed the paper and jumped up. "This isn't doing any good. Come on, let's get the garbage."

Supergranny had given us the job of cleaning up after Old Jellie. She'd let us wait until today just in case he was still lurking around in the shadows last night.

Cleaning up a garbage can that has been attacked by a bear could have been a Class A mess. But this wasn't too bad, because the can had been empty except for the leftovers from the picnic lunch we'd brought on the trip.

We were throwing everything back in the can when Angela grabbed my wrist.

"What's that?"

"Just an old wadded up piece of lined yellow paper," I said, tossing it into the can.

She grabbed it and sat down on the stoop.

"Strange," she said, smoothing it out. "Very strange. When I threw out our garbage last night, the can was totally empty."

"And we didn't have any lined yellow paper . . ." I said slowly. "So where did this come from?"

We stared at the smoothed-out paper.

Two columns of numbers and one word were scribbled on it in ink. The word was "Peppers."

Pinned to the upper right-hand corner was a tiny metal boot.

"Hmmmmm," Angela muttered. "Hmmmmm before. Where? Hmmmmmmmm." Then she stared at the swinging bridge and muttered some more. "Hmmmmm muttermuttermutter. Wherrrrre muttermuttermutter."

Then she screamed, jumped up and raced into the kitchen.

"JOSHUA! The book! That's where I've seen these numbers before!"

I raced after her. I had no idea why she'd flipped out, but I wasn't about to sit calmly on the porch while she tore around the kitchen yelling, " *'NANCY DREW,' 'CLUE IN THE DIARY,' 'JUSTIN MORGAN HAD A HORSE,' 'REBECCA OF SUNNYBROOK FARM!'* "

I found her in the corner going through the bookcase like a crazy person. "WhereisitwhereisitwhereISit?" She tapped each book as she yelled its title. " *'The Lion, The Witch and The Wardrobe,' 'Charlotte's Web,' 'The Wind in the Willows'* — Joshua, for Pete's sake — HELP."

Down the row she went: " *'My Friend Flicka,' 'Little House on the Prairie,' 'Hardy Boys Detective Handbook' 'Nancy Drew,' 'Nancy Drew,' 'Nancy Drew,' 'Hans Brinker.'*

"Where IS it?" she screamed, more and more and more like a crazy person.

"It was HERE. LAST NIGHT. RIGHT NEXT TO 'HANS BRINKER.' SOMEONE BROKE IN HERE AND STOLE THAT BOOK RIGHT FROM UNDER OUR NOSES!"

"You mean this?" I asked, picking up a book from under the chair where she'd been reading the night before. "You didn't put it back."

"Oh," she said, snatching it out of my hand.

It was "Five Little Peppers."

Triumphantly, she pulled a folded, faded sheet of lined yellow paper from the middle of the book.

Above the fold were two rows of numbers:

100,136	107,211
101,31	108,119
102,25	104,14
102,25	105,16
103,37	100,136
104,14	101,31
105,216	106,18
106,18	100,136
	110,118

Below the fold were two rows of letters:

C	N
O	D
B	E
B	R
L	C
E	O
R	U
U	C
	H

"See!" she said. "Except for the fact that it doesn't have "Peppers" written on it and doesn't have a little metal boot pinned to it and has two rows of letters on it and hasn't been all crumpled up and is faded . . . it's EXACTLY like the paper we found with the garbage!"

"Yeah," I said. "Except for that, they're identical. But so what?"

"So what?" she mimicked to me, rolling her eyes to the ceiling. " 'So what?' he asks.

"It's a coded message, that's 'so what,' Joshua. Someone is trying to tell us something. We've got to crack this code! Fast!"

Just then a figure loomed in the doorway.

It was Boots.

7

"What's that?" he asked sharply.

He was frowning and didn't seem at all like the jolly, booming-voiced Boots of the night before.

" *'Five Little Peppers,'* " Angela said airily, pretending to mark her place with the folded paper. "An old book of Mom's." She pointed to "Gwinn Bowen" written inside the cover.

"It's about five kids whose father is dead and mother is a poor seamstress. They say 'My whockety!' when they're surprised. Did you and Mom say 'My whockety' in the old days?"

He laughed, more like the Boots of last night.

"Nope. 'My whockety' must have been before my time."

"How'd the Ferrari drive?" I asked, trying to push the subject as far away from the coded message in the book as I could.

"Like a dream," he said.

"Did anybody shoot at you?" Angela asked.

"Nope, I guess they didn't know it was me." He laughed. "Nobody expects Plain Old Boots to be tooling into town in a red Ferrari. It's a great disguise."

I started remembering how much I liked him. Maybe Supergranny and Angela were going off the deep end — talking about smelling a rat and all.

We were *supposed* to be *helping* him. Mom's favorite cousin! Our host!

What kind of guests were we anyway, talking about him behind his back? Hiding coded messages from him? Maybe the rat Supergranny smelled was us!

Just then Supergranny and Vannie breezed into the kitchen with Shackleford and Chesterton.

They looked grim.

"Did you hear the bad news?" Supergranny asked. "Vannie heard it on her Walkman while we were picking blackberries. Haji Jamad's limousine didn't arrive at the Greenbrier this morning.

"The ambassador is missing."

Boots froze. He seemed too surprised to move, much less say, "My whockety!"

So Supergranny took charge.

The plan had been for Boots to leave at noon for his secret 3 p.m. meeting with Jamad at the Greenbrier.

The only secret part, of course, was the meeting with Boots. The entire world and international press knew Jamad had a 4 p.m. meeting at the Greenbrier with a U.S. State Department undersecretary.

"I suggest you go to the Greenbrier as planned, Boots," Supergranny said briskly. "See what you can find out. Take the Ferrari and leave us the pickup keys. I might take the kids to the Devil Park Lodge for lunch."

Before you could say "The ambassador is missing" ten times, I had his suitcase in the Ferrari, Supergranny had the pickup keys in her purse, and Boots was backing out to the road.

"I'll be home in the morning," he called huskily. "Are you sure you'll be all right?"

"Positive," Supergranny said. "You just find out what you can about Jamad. We'll hold the fort here."

He waved and was off.

One thing for sure: If Supergranny smelled a rat about Boots, she certainly wouldn't trust him with her beloved Ferrari.

Would she?

*   *   *   *   *   *

The minute the Ferrari pulled out of the yard, Angela whipped out the faded, coded message from the 'Five Little Peppers' book.

"Exhibit A" she said grandly, handing it to Supergranny.

Then she pulled the crumpled paper we'd found in the garbage from her pocket.

"Exhibit B," she said with a flourish.

Supergranny tilted her head and peered at the first paper through her bifocals. Then she peered at the second. Then she held both in front of her and looked from one to the other and back again.

"Where did you find these?" she asked quietly.

Angela and I took turns explaining about finding the new, crumpled paper in the garbage, then the older, faded paper in the book.

"Angela thought it was stolen, but she'd just left it under her chair," I explained. "She totally flipped out, racing around the kitchen screaming that the book was stolen and —"

"Never mind," Angela cut in. "You're wasting time."

Supergranny put both papers on the kitchen table, sat down and stared at them some more.

"Let's see that book, Angela," she said.

Angela handed her *Five Little Peppers*," and she leafed through the pages. Then stared at the papers. Then leafed through more pages.

"Conference," she said.

We all sat down around the table, except for Shackleford and Chesterton, who sat under it.

She pulled papers and pencils out of her purse and passed them around. She glanced at her watch.

"I only have time to go through this once," she said. "So please pay strict attention.

"Operation 'Find Haji Jamad' starts in ten minutes."

"So if someone is trying to get a message to us we have just ten minutes to figure it out.

"First, ARE YOU POSITIVE Paper 2 wasn't already in the can when you threw out the garbage last night?"

"Absolutely," Angela said. "The can was totally empty."

"And are you positive one of us didn't throw it out?" Supergranny asked.

"Absolutely," Angela said. "I threw out the garbage. And

I was the only one on the back porch last night."

"What about Boots?" Supergranny said. "Maybe he threw it out."

"But Boots wasn't out back last night," Vannie put in. "Unless he went out after we were asleep."

"Impossible," I said. "I was on that couch all night. I would have known if he'd passed me to go outside."

"And I was in the kitchen when he got up this morning . . ." Supergranny mused. "As soon as he drank his coffee, he went out the front door, started the Ferrari and left for town."

"So . . ." she went on. "Who put the message in the garbage?"

All of us stared at the crumpled, lined, yellow paper.

"Old Jellie?" Vannie asked.

"A messenger bearing news?" Angela joked.

Everybody laughed. It was ridiculous. Messenger pigeons were one thing, but who'd ever heard of a messenger bear?

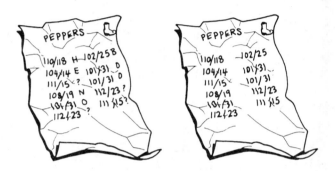

8

It didn't take long to crack the code.

To review, the crumpled paper had three things:

1. The word "Peppers."
2. A small boot pinned to the upper right-hand corner.
3. Two rows of numbers.

First we took a hard look at the old message Angela found in the book. We figured the numbers at the top must match the letters at the bottom. That meant the first number (100/136) stood for the first letter "C." The second number (101/31) stood for the second letter "O." And so on, down the line.

Then we matched the numbers on the new message with the numbers on the old. Most were the same, so we were able to come up with all but four letters.

That may sound murky as mud, but check out the messages on the next page and you'll see what I mean.

Old message:

100,136	C	107,211	N	C	N
101,31	O	108,119	D	O	D
102,25	B	104,14	E	B	E
102,25	B	105,16	R	B	R
103,37	L	100,136	C	L	C
104,14	E	101,31	O	E	O
105,216	R	106,18	U	R	U
106,18	U	100,136	C	U	C
		110,118	H		

New message:

110,118	102,25
104,14	101,31
111,15	101,31
108,19	112,23
101,31	111,15
112,23	

Here's what we got:

110,118	H	102,25	B
104,14	E	101,31	O
111,15	?	101,31	O
107,211	N	112,23	?
101,31	O	111,15	?
112,23	?		

"HE NO BOO?" Vannie said, scrunching her nose.

"Oh, great," Angela said sarcastically. "THAT will lead us straight to the vanished ambassador."

"Could it be a foreign language?" I asked. "Balkhastani

or something? After all, 'Cobbleru Ndercouch' doesn't make a heck of a lot of sense, either."

"Oh for heaven's sake," Supergranny said. "It's clear as a telephone book. Use your noodles."

We looked at the message again.

"I think I've got it!" Angela said. "But I hope not. . . ."

I knew what she meant because I thought I had it, too. And if I was right, we had a Major Bigtime Problem.

Angela handed me *Five Little Peppers.*

"We need to find the letter for 111/15," she said. "The first number is probably a page number, so find page 111."

I turned to page 111.

"Maybe the second number is the number of the letter on the page . . . so count to the 15th letter."

"It's 'i,' " I said.

We tried it:

110,118	H	102,25	B
104,14	E	101,31	O
111,15	I	101,31	O
107,211	N	112,23	?
101,31	O	111,15	I
112,23	?		

"HEINO BOO I?" Vannie said, rescrunching her nose.

"Drat," Angela said. "That can't be right. Maybe 'l' means first line and '5' means fifth letter. Try that."

I looked at the first line on page 111 and counted to the 5th letter. It was "s."

And we got this:

110,118	H	102,25	B
104,14	E	101,31	O
111,15	S	101,31	O
107,211	N	112,23	?
101,31	O	111,15	S
112,23	?		

"HESNO BOO S?" Vannie said.

Angela and I looked at each other. "All we need is 112/23," she said solemnly.

I turned to page 112, looked at line 2 and counted to the third letter. It was "t."

"HESNOT BOOTS," Vannie said slowly.

"I'm afraid not," Supergranny said. "The real Boots called us for help. But the man we met last night, and the man who just drove off in my Ferrari . . ."

"*He's not Boots*," Vannie whispered.

9

Operation "Find Haji Jamad" started five minutes later.

Except now it was Operation "Find Haji Jamad and Real Boots."

"But I don't understand," Vannie kept saying. "He looked exactly like my picture of Boots on the beach in Argentina."

"And he knew so much about us. And Mom. And almost everything," Angela added.

"And he was such a nice guy," I said.

Supergranny sighed. "I know. It's hard to believe. He's a clever actor. Tall, husky build like the real Boots. Well-briefed. Right clothes. Right beard. It fooled me for a while, too."

"But, remember, none of us had ever actually met Boots. And since the phone line was fuzzy, we'd never heard his voice clearly . . . and some things just didn't add up."

"Like when he fished around to find out what we knew about Haji Jamad," Angela said.

"Right," said Supergranny.

"Then tried to back out of telling us," Angela said.

"And didn't remember Mom yelling 'Snake, snake,' " Vannie said.

"And thought Buenos Aires was in Brazil," I said.

"Right, right, right," Supergranny said.

"BUT WHY?" the three of us asked together. "And how?"

"Hop in the pickup, and I'll explain my theory," Supergranny answered, grabbing a roll of aluminum foil from a kitchen drawer. "Remember, it's just a theory. At this point, I can't be sure."

Shackleford and Chesterton jumped into the back of the pickup as the rest of us crowded into the cab.

Supergranny slid behind the wheel, shoved the gear-shift into first and the truck rattled up the mountain road toward the rock cliff.

"Your theory?" Vannie shouted as we bumped along.

"Someone is trying to overthrow the Balkhastani democratic government and wants Jamad out of the way," Supergranny shouted back. "Spies found out he was going to meet here secretly with Boots and kidnapped them both.

"When they discovered that Boots had already alerted us, they sent a cleverly trained agent to pose as Boots to throw us off track."

"*IF* my theory is correct, our job is to save Jamad, the real Boots, Balkhastani democracy — and my beautiful, red Ferrari!"

*　　　*　　　*　　　*　　　*　　　*

But why had she let Fake Boots drive off in her Ferrari? Why did she just hand over the keys when she already suspected him?

"Simple, my dear Watsons," she explained, as the pickup lurched to a halt beside the rock cliff path.

"To trick him. To make him think we'd bought his little act. To give us time to find Real Boots."

"But your Ferrari," Angela said softly.

"Your wonderful Ferrari," Vannie echoed.

"I know, I know," she said impatiently. "Don't dwell on it; it will give me a headache. Every time I think of him pulling out of that yard — AGGGHHHHH!" — she pounded the steering wheel with her fist.

Then she laughed. It seemed to calm her down.

"But, after all, it's only a car. A wonderful car, but only a car. What's one little Ferrari if it means we save Real Boots and Haji Jamad?"

That was true. But could we save them? Without the Ferrari? Six hundred miles from Supergranny's workshop-office-laboratory-playroom-garage?

You may already know about Supergranny's workshop-office-laboratory-playroom-garage. If so, you probably know I think it's the best room in the world. I think you could look for 137 years to find a better room and come up with zip.

But it's a real shock the first time you see it.

At least, it shocked me.

The day we moved in from Cleveland, Shackleford went goofy and ran off, and I went next door to Mrs. Oglepop's (alias Supergranny) to dog hunt.

After I found Shackleford, Mrs. Oglepop invited Vannie and me in for snickerdoodle cookies and lemonade. Of course, we thought we were just in your typical old lady's typical kitchen.

At first.

Until we stumbled into her secret room behind the fireplace.

That's where she keeps the Ferrari, Chesterton, the helicopter pad, swimming pool, vending machines, world maps and most of her crime-fighting equipment. Because, as we soon found out, Supergranny is a world-class crime fighter.

Although she may not look it, she loooooooves to fight crime.

And hates to waste time.

"Let's move it," she said briskly, pulling a pair of binoculars out of her purse and handing them to me.

"We'll use Plan 432BZ."

The first goal of Plan 432BZ was to find the spot where the limousine and chain of Fords had disappeared into the woods.

Why?

Because Supergranny smelled a connection.

"It's too big a coincidence to ignore," she explained in the pickup.

"Yesterday we saw a strange limo disappear into some

of the most rugged terrain in the United States.

"Then we learned that Ambassador Jamad had planned a secret meeting with Boots, who lives down the road.

"Today we heard Ambassador Jamad had disappeared.

"Any nincompoop would suspect it might be Ambassador Jamad's limo. At any rate, it's too big a coincidence to ignore."

"But, Supergranny, you always tell us not to rely on coincidence," Angela pointed out. "You ALWAYS say that's the first rule of crime fighting."

"Exactly," Supergranny said. "And the key word is RELY. Don't RELY on coincidence.

"But the second rule of crime fighting is don't IGNORE coincidence when it hits you on the head. Especially a coincidence as big as a boulder.

"Sooooo . . . we've got to find the spot that limo disappeared, and it's not going to be as easy as it sounds because I wasn't kidding when I said we're smack in the middle of some of the ruggedest territory in America.

"First, we'll divide into teams. Angela and Joshua, you take Chesterton to the top of the rock cliff. Vannie, Shackleford and I will take the pickup into the valley. You find the spot and guide us to it.

"We'll stop every ten minutes to signal, starting at — " she glanced at her watch — "12:10 p.m. It's now noon, Eastern Daylight Time. Does everybody have noon?"

We all checked our watches. Everybody had noon except me. I had 11 a.m., because I hadn't changed from Illinois' Central Daylight Time. While I reset my watch,

Supergranny gave us instructions and handed out the rest of our equipment.

Then Angela and I hopped out of the pickup, grabbed Chesterton and started up the overgrown trail to the rock cliff.

The pickup rattled off in a cloud of flying pebbles.

From the back of the truck, Shackleford gazed at us, her hair whipping wildly in the wind.

10

Our timing was too tight.

It was almost 12:10 before Angela, Chesterton and I even made it to the top of the rock cliff. I could just picture Supergranny down below, waiting for us to signal. And here we were, still huffing and puffing and scrambling up the cliff.

As soon as we made it, I grabbed the binoculars and scanned the valley.

At first everything was just a green and gray blur.

It took me several minutes to even find the road. It wound around, disappeared under us, wound out again.

And I couldn't see the old red pickup anywhere.

"Well, we've missed the 12:10 check," I said.

"No sweat," Angela said. "We'll make the 12:20. Put your finger in this knot."

She was sitting on the rock tying Supergranny's red, white and blue silk Gucci scarf to a stick to make a signal flag.

Supergranny's friend Ms. Richmont[1] had brought the Gucci scarf to her from Italy, and she took it everywhere. It was part of the crucial equipment she'd given us down in the pickup.

Angela finished the signal flag at 12:18 and stood up beside me. I'd gone back to binocular scanning as soon as my finger was out of the knot.

"Have you spotted it?" she asked.

Slowly, I moved the binoculars over the miles of green treetops.

"Nope," I answered.

Somewhere down there Supergranny was waiting for us to direct her to the spot where the limo had disappeared. We knew it was impossible to find it from the ground. Our only chance was to find it from up here where we'd seen it before.

But I was beginning to think it was impossible from up here, too.

Slowly I rescanned the valley.

Treetops, treetops, rock. Treetops, treetops, rock. Treetops, treetops, rock. Hopeless, hopeless, hopeless.

---

1. More about Myrtle Witherspoon Richmont in "Supergranny 1: The Mystery of the Shrunken Heads."

Even worse, it was hard to concentrate because Chesterton had the fidgets. He was racing around the top of the rock cliff in circles, beeping and whirring and jumping up and down. Then he jumped onto a thin ledge, turned off his lights and beeper and just stared out at the valley. One more inch and over he'd go, smack into three thousand feet of underbrush.

He was making me so nervous I could spit.

"All we need is for Chesterton to take a header off this cliff," I said to Angela. "Can't you keep an eye on him while I try to focus these blasted binoculars?"

"I can't. It's 12:20 and I have to signal," Angela said.

She was right. And sure enough, far down below a tiny pickup had just pulled into view around a curve. It stopped and a tiny Supergranny and Vannie jumped out and waved.

What'll I tell them?" Angela asked.

"Tell them we don't know yet," I shouted over Chesterton's whirring and beeping. He'd started up again.

"What?" Angela shouted. The *xx*@! robot was making so much *xx*@! noise she couldn't hear me.

"TELL THEM WE DON'T KNOW YET!" I shouted, peering through the binoculars at the tiny Supergranny and Vannie.

Angela waved the Gucci flag slowly to the right, back to the left, and repeated. Then she lowered it. Then she did the same thing again.

It meant we hadn't found the spot yet.

Two waves to the right, a stop, then two more waves to the right meant they were to drive farther up the road.

49

Two waves to the left, a stop, then two more waves to the left meant they should drive back down the road.

We'd worked out the signals in the pickup.

Through the binoculars I watched Supergranny wave both arms over her head, the signal that she'd gotten our message. She and Vannie hopped back in the pickup and took off.

"That's it for ten minutes," Angela said. "Let me look while you corral Chesterton."

I handed her the binoculars and lunged for Chesterton. He was too fast for me. Chesterton can change directions faster than you can flip on a TV.

He zipped around the top of that cliff like a greyhound around a track. Lights flashing, beeper beeping, sensor whirring. Then he LEAPED back onto that thin ledge and stopped. He turned off his lights and beeper and stood still, staring at the valley.

"Chesterton, you get back here," I yelled. I wasn't about to crawl out on that thin ledge after him. "Get back here NOW."

He just stood there, stubborn as stone.

"Ignore him," Angela whispered, still peering through the binoculars.

He heard her, and that REALLY set him off.

Instantly, he sprang off the ledge, lights and beepers at full go. He landed right on Angela's foot and nipped her on the ankle.

It was war.

She screamed and was after him. Round and round they went. Blinking lights, screaming, beeping, whirring.

I just stood there like a golf caddy, holding the Gucci flagpole.

"Now calm down," I said, hoping they didn't fall off the cliff and that if they did, they didn't take me with them.

"This isn't finding Boots and Haji and the Ferrari," I said. "This isn't saving Balkhastani democracy." I said.

They didn't pay the slightest attention.

Chesterton LEAPED back onto the ledge, came to a dead stop and turned off his lights and beeper.

"Give me that," Angela snarled, grabbing the Gucci flag from me. She stretched out on her stomach and tried to scoop him back from the ledge with the Gucci flagpole.

Suddenly she froze and stared out at the valley.

"Joshua," she whispered, "give me those binoculars." Still lying on her stomach, she sighted the binoculars right across Chesterton's sensor.

"I apologize, Chesterton," she said softly. "No wonder you bit me on the ankle."

She looked up at me and grinned. "Chesterton's found it. He's been trying to tell us. His computer memory recorded the spot where the limo disappeared."

11

We were ready and waiting for the 12:30 p.m. check.

"Good night, look where they are," Angela said. "They're halfway to Ohio."

She was exaggerating, of course. But the pickup HAD stopped on the other side of a bridge, miles past the spot where the limo had disappeared.

It was so far I couldn't even see Supergranny and Vannie — just something moving around in the pickup that had to be Shackleford. But Angela could see them with the binoculars.

"They're ready. Give them the signal," she said.

I waved the Gucci flag to the left and back to the center twice, stopped and did it again — the signal to come back this way.

"They got it," Angela said. "Supergranny's waving her

arms over her head."

We watched the pickup turn around, then head back our way over the bridge. It wound in and out of the hills and right past the limo spot.

"STOP, STOP, STOP!" Angela yelled, but of course Supergranny couldn't hear her.

"Good night, look where she's going," Angela muttered. "She'll be halfway to Virginia by the 12:40 p.m. check."

She was exaggerating again, but the pickup WAS already way past the secret road.

"This is going to take all day," I said. "And I'm getting hungry. Are you?"

"Starved, but forget food. At this rate we'll never eat again," Angela said. "Wait! Hang on! She's stopping! She's not going to wait until 12:40 p.m. Quick, signal to go back up the road."

Before I'd even finished the two waves to the right, Supergranny hopped back in the pickup and turned it around.

She drove about a quarter mile, then stopped again.

I signaled her to go farther.

This time she barely passed it.

Angela and Chesterton jumped up and down with excitement as I quickly signaled twice to the left.

The pickup turned around again and drove about thirty feet.

"They're within ten feet of it," Angela said excitedly. "Tell them they're there, but to go slightly farther."

I looked at her blankly. "We don't have a signal for that," I said.

"IMPROVISE, YOU TURKEY," Angela shouted, still peering through the binoculars.

I held the Gucci straight up, moving it slowly in circles — our signal for "That's the spot." Then I waved it to the right twice, stopped, and waved it again. Then I repeated the whole thing.

It was my improvised signal for "You're almost there, just walk a few feet farther."

If the pickup started up again, I'd know they didn't understand.

"IT WORKED!" Angela yelled. "She's signaling that she got it. Nice work, Joshua!"

A tiny Supergranny, Vannie and Shackleford walked along the road. Every two feet they'd duck into the trees to look for the secret road, then come back out again.

"So close, so close, so close," Angela whispered, watching through the binoculars. Suddenly Chesterton's sensor whirled like a propeller.

"THEY'VE GOT IT!" Angela shouted.

She tossed me the binoculars. By the time I focused, the three of them were racing toward the truck. Slowly, the pickup lurched toward the spot. Then Supergranny and Vannie climbed into the truck bed and Supergranny boosted Vannie to the truck roof.

Quickly, Vannie tied three strips of the aluminum foil we'd taken from Boots' kitchen to a tree branch. We hoped nobody would see them marking the spot or notice the foil that high above eye level.

The idea was to mark the spot with something shiny so we could find it again that night . . . in the dark.

*　　　*　　　*　　　*　　　*　　　*

The Devil Mountain Lodge restaurant had windows on three sides overlooking mountainsides covered with pink and white and purple flowers.

"Rhododendron," Supergranny explained. "The West Virginia state flower. Whole canyons and jungles of rhododendron. All my life I've dreamed of being here when they were in bloom, but I've never made it until now. We sure hit it lucky this time."

"Lucky, except that Boots is missing," Angela said.

"And Fake Boots has your Ferrari," Vannie said.

"And Balkhastani democracy may be on the skids," I said.

"Shhhh," Supergranny whispered. "Pretend we're tourists enjoying the view. Pretend it's just an ordinary day. Don't let on we're searching for a missing ambassador.

"Besides, I meant lucky except for that," she said, tearing herself away from the view to look at the menu. "Eat up. Anything you want. Heaven only knows if or when we'll have supper."

We'd headed for the lodge as soon as she picked up Angela, Chesterton and me from the bottom of the rock cliff. A senior citizens' tour bus from Charleston had arrived the same time we did, and the place was jumping.

Supergranny had already met and exchanged addresses and other information with half of them while we were waiting for our table.

We knew they were from Charleston, West Virginia, would be staying overnight at the lodge and would leave early the next morning for the Grand Ole Opry in Tennessee.

They knew we were from Illinois, our mother was from West Virginia and we were visiting a cousin down the road.

One of them, a frail-looking, retired schoolteacher with dark red hair and about a hundred rings on her fingers, leaned over from the next table to talk to us after we ordered. Her name was Annie Scott Woods, and, as we soon learned, WASN'T frail.

"You HAVE taken the trails, haven't you?" she asked.

"What trails?" Angela replied.

"Why, right down there, dear. In fact, two of the best trails start right outside the restaurant and go down into the valley and circle back up again."

"I hear there are bears down there," I said.

"In fact, we met a bear from down there," Vannie said.

Annie Scott Woods and the three others at her table pulled their chairs closer while we told them about Old Jellie. At least Fake Boots had called the bear "Old Jellie." Maybe that had been a lie, too.

If it was, Annie Scott Woods had heard it.

"Oh, Jellie won't hurt you," she said. "I spend a week in a cabin up here with my grandchildren every year. Last summer, Old Jellie sneaked up behind my grandson — you met my grandson, Frank —"

We nodded. He was their bus driver; we'd met him on the way in. "— sneaked up behind Frank and snatched a hamburger he was cooking right off the grill."

Everybody laughed, including Annie. "It's funny now, but it didn't strike Frank quite so funny at the time."

"I suppose the bears avoid the trails to stay away from the people," Angela said.

56

"No, not really," Annie answered. "In fact, they seem to like the trails. Once last summer I happened on a bear scratching his back on a trail sign. And one of the signs has tooth marks on the corners where a bear sharpened its teeth." She bared her teeth and tapped them for emphasis.

"I can take you right to it. As soon as we eat, I'll meet you at the start of the Rhododendron Trail."

Angela, Vannie and I weren't crazy about the idea. If the bears liked the Rhododendron Trail THAT much, we'd just as soon let them have it.

"Oh, no, thank you anyway," Vannie said.

"We don't want to impose," Angela said.

"I'm a little tired," I said.

"Wonderful! It's a deal," Supergranny said.

"Marvelous," Annie said, leaning closer. "It will give me a break from the others," she whispered. "They're lovely people, the salt of the earth, but after being cooped up on a bus, we could use a break from each other." She rolled her eyes for emphasis.

Supergranny nodded.

Angela, Vannie and I each took a deep breath, blew it out, and stared at the bear-infested valley.

Just what we needed in our lives — another daredevil old lady!

12

The Rhododendron Trail was marked with green circles painted on trees and rocks. It was so narrow we had to go single file.

Annie Scott Woods led, of course.

Then came Angela with Shackleford on the leash, Vannie with Chesterton in her backpack, and me with a long bear-fighting stick I'd picked up, just in case. Supergranny brought up the rear.

Why waste time traipsing down the Rhododendron Trail when we had to find Real Boots and the missing ambassador?

That's what I wanted to know.

"Shouldn't we be looking for Boots and Haji?" I whispered to Supergranny over my shoulder.

"We can't check out the secret road until dark anyway,"

she whispered back. "And the better I know a territory, the better I like it.

"Besides, how often do we get the chance to hike through a jungle of blooming rhododendron?"

True.

Everywhere you looked there were steep walls of pink flowers with the sun shining right through the petals. Some of the petals had already fallen and covered the ground like confetti. I'd never seen anything quite like it and, best of all, there was no sign of Old Jellie and friends.

Except, of course, the tooth-marked trail sign that Annie Scott Woods was busting to show us.

"See the bear's tooth marks," she said when we got there, tapping the gouges in the sign with her long, pointed fingernails. "Tooth marks," she said, baring her teeth and tapping them again for emphasis.

You could hardly hear her for the rushing sound around us.

"What's that?" Vannie asked. "It sounds like heavy traffic."

"Devil Creek Falls," Annie Scott Woods said. "It's just a small waterfall, but very pretty. It's on another trail; you can't see it from this trail, but I know a shortcut. Come on!"

Before you could say "Mountaineers are always free," the West Virginia state motto, she ducked behind a rhododendron bush and disappeared. Angela and Shackleford were right behind her.

"After them, Vannie!" Supergranny called from the rear.

And that's how we learned the shortcut between Rhododendron Trail and Devil Creek Falls. The shortcut that saved our necks.

Thank you, Annie Scott Woods, for showing us that shortcut.

Thank you, thank you, thank you!

*   *   *   *   *   *

We all sat down to rest on the bridge at the base of the falls.

Nobody said anything for a minute because it was so interesting watching the creek divide into streams to pour over the rocks.

It all swirled together again under the bridge, then bounced on its way and out of sight between the trees.

Then Angela cleared her throat. "I guess this is as good a time as any," she said.

"Time for what, dear?" Supergranny asked.

I groaned. I knew. So did Vannie.

"The Hatfields and McCoys," Vannie said. "The feud."

"You promised," Angela reminded her, "that I could give everyone a complete blow-by-blow report today."

"Yes, of course, it slipped my mind," Supergranny said with a laugh. "But we have a big night ahead of us, and Annie has to get back to her tour — so how about doing a three-in-one?"

A three-in-one is a Supergranny invention to help Angela boil down her reports. It's a complete oral report done in three sentences in only one minute.

Otherwise, she could go on for years. Once she got an

A+ on a report about President Franklin D. Roosevelt and was DETERMINED to tell Vannie and me the whole thing.

She started the first day of summer vacation and by the Fourth of July, Roosevelt hadn't even been elected to his second term. I knew Roosevelt was elected to four terms, and I was desperate. My entire summer vacation was drowning in Franklin Roosevelt.

We had to give her my last five dollars and Vannie's Whitney Houston tapes to get her to stop.

"You mean you want me to tell about a fifty-year feud in only three sentences?" Angela asked. "In just one minute?"

"It's good discipline, honey," Supergranny said, then explained the three-in-one to Annie Scott Woods.

"And speak up, dear," Annie Scott Woods said. "So our ears won't come out on their stalks trying to hear you above the sound of the falls."

"And stand up straight, look at the whites of our eyes and speak from the diaphragm," she added, patting her stomach for emphasis. "That's what I always told my students, 'Don't ruin a good speech by being mealy-mouthed.' "

Supergranny pulled out her stopwatch and tossed it to me for the countdown.

"Ten, nine, eight, seven, six, five, four, three, two, one, GO!" I shouted.

She stared at the whites of our eyes and was off:

"The Hatfields lived on the West Virginia side of the Tug River, and the McCoys lived on the Kentucky side, and according to many accounts their feud began with a fight over a pig in about 1873."

"A pig?" Vannie said. "A fifty-year feud over a pig?"

"Eighteen seconds," I said.

"In those days it was common to brand your pigs with a notch in their ears, then let them run wild until they were fat enough to slaughter, and in this case, a Hatfield killed what the McCoys claimed was a McCoy pig and although the fighting died down after a while, it started up again when Johnse Hatfield fell in love with Rose Anne McCoy but his mean old dad, Devil Anse, wouldn't let them marry and before you knew it there was worse fighting and people were killed on both sides, and even though governors of both states sent in soldiers and said they wanted to break it up, fighting kept popping up again —"

"Forty seconds," I said.

"— until finally Devil Anse, who lived in a rough old fort way back in the mountains, got religion and calmed down in his old age, and the new generation thought constant fighting was boring and old-fashioned, not to mention dangerous, so they went out into the world and got good educations and became teachers and sheriffs and governors and things like that instead!"

"TIME!" I yelled, as she finished with a flourish, bowed to us and curtsied to Devil Creek Falls.

"You know, my father met Devil Anse Hatfield," Annie Scott Woods said as we stopped applauding. "When he came to Charleston for his moonshine whiskey trial in 1889, he'd stand around on street corners and people would crowd around to talk to him. He loved the attention."

"What did your father think of him?" I asked.

"Not much," Annie said. "Many of the Hatfields were fine folks, of course, and some big-city newspaper reporters tried to make out that Devil Anse was fine underneath, too. They thought he was cute and colorful and kidded themselves he was a simple, warmhearted rustic underneath.

"But my Dad thought otherwise. He said Devil Anse might be colorful and cute, but underneath he was a cruel, self-centered ignoramus.

"Devil Anse didn't go, you know, the night the Hatfields raided the McCoy cabin in 1888. He sent the younger Hatfield fellows while he hid at home. They set fire to the McCoy cabin, then shot the women as they came out to get buckets of water to douse the flames.

"There wasn't anything cute or colorful about it. Or about Devil Anse either, if you ask me."

"It started over a pig?" Vannie asked again. "A fifty-year feud *over a pig*?"

13

Supergranny made us take naps when we got back to Boots' house. Or at least pretend to take naps.

"We'll need all our strength and wits when we search that secret road tonight," she said. "So get as much rest as you can."

I was pretty tired after not sleeping all night on Boots' lumpy couch, but trying to nap on the same couch wasn't the answer.

The lumpiness didn't keep me awake as much as the questions buzzing through my brain:

Had Real Boots and Haji been in that limousine yesterday?

Who was driving that chain of Fords? Cutthroat Balkhastani crooks?

And who had left the "He's not Boots" coded message in the garbage?

Every time I almost drifted off, old bearded Devil Anse would pop into my head. Then he'd turn into a Balkhastani kidnapper riding an elephant. That would set off more questions.

Who shot at Fake Boots last night? Who *was* Fake Boots?

But one question kept chasing away all the rest.

What was at the end of the secret road on Devil Mountain?

* * * * * *

I guess I finally did sleep, because suddenly the pendulum clock on the mantle was chiming "eight" and the room was filled with shadows.

I pulled on my jeans and long-sleeved black turtleneck. The long sleeves were hot, but that was a small price to pay. The idea was to blend into the night so some Balkhastani cutthroat couldn't see me.

Supergranny, Angela and Vannie were already in their black clothes in the kitchen, eating peanut butter and jelly sandwiches. I joined them and grabbed a sandwich, while Supergranny went over the details of Plan 437XKG. Everybody was quiet, even Shackleford and Chesterton.

At 8:40 p.m. she looked at her watch, then stood up and gazed out the kitchen window where we'd seen Old Jellie the night before.

"It will be plenty dark enough by the time we get there," she said. "Let's move it."

We all piled into the pickup for the short drive past the rock cliff and back down the valley to the secret road.

Supergranny turned off the headlights about a mile before we got there, then pulled off the side of the road about a quarter of a mile away.

"We have to hoof it from here," she whispered. "It's too risky to take the pickup any closer."

Once again, we walked single file — this time along the valley road.

"Team One, look for the aluminum foil markers," Supergranny whispered.

"Team Two, watch for cars, Balkhastani criminals, holes in the road, bears and assorted other wild animals."

She, Vannie and Chesterton were Team One.

They walked along with their noses (and Chesterton's sensor) pointed up and to the left, scanning the tree branches for the foil Vannie had tied up there.

That left Angela, Shackleford and me the job of watching out for everything else, including chuckholes and dropoffs Team One might fall into or over because they weren't watching where they were going.

This went on for some time, and I was beginning to think the foil had blown off or been eaten by crows or spotted by Balkhastani cutthroats when Supergranny stopped short and we all crashed into her.

She pointed over our heads and grinned.

Sure enough, little bits of foil were glimmering up there in the moonlight.

Supergranny dropped to a crouch, then ducked into the woods through the underbrush. The rest of us followed, with Shackleford behind the heels of Angela's tennis shoes and me behind Shackleford.

The underbrush was thick with scratchy branches, and I wasn't crazy about the scurrying sounds of birds and small animals as we walked.

On the other hand, I wasn't crazy about going back out to the highway by myself, either. So I followed Shackleford's rump as best I could and soon the branches thinned out and we were in a clearing.

Supergranny switched on her flashlight, risking a light to see if we were on the right track. Sure enough, we were in the middle of a narrow dirt road. She quickly switched off the beam.

"Teams," she whispered. She, Vannie and Chesterton took the left side of the road. Team Two — Angela, Shackleford and I — took the right.

We moved in a sort of stooping walk along the edges of the secret road. Back in the woods, the trees and curve of the mountain cut off the moonlight, making it so dark I couldn't see Team One across the narrow road. The black clothes really did the job.

Plan 437XKG called for stopping every ten feet to signal like a katydid, a sort of grasshopper that makes "Katydid, Katydid" sounds.

We had to guess how far ten feet was, of course, but that was easy: It's exactly the length of my room at home.

Each time we'd stop and wait for Supergranny's Katydid signal. Then Angela would katydid back. Then we'd do it again, to make sure we weren't getting mixed up with the 148 million real katydids katydidding their heads off all around us.

It was slow, but it worked.

On and up we went. On and up. Onanduponanduponandup.

Finally the road leveled off, then dipped gradually into a hidden hollow, tucked in the mountains.

Pale, silvery moonlight had found its way into the hollow, revealing a small cabin.

Lamplight glowed from its window. Smoke wafted from its chimney.

And parked beside the broken front steps was a dirty red Ferrari.

14

It looked like the loneliest little cabin in the world.

Angela and I just stood, fascinated by the eerie silence and ghostly moonlight. Even Shackleford stood like stone, forgetting to pant.

Then we noticed the movement on the porch.

A man stood up and stretched, picked up something long and thin and rested it in the bend of his arm. He stepped off the porch stiffly, as though his knees hurt, then circled the cabin counter-clockwise. He came back to the porch, leaned the long thin thing against the railing, sat back down on the top step and rubbed his knees.

I thought I knew what the long thin thing was, but hoped I was wrong. I hoped it was only a bear-fighting stick like I'd carried on the Rhododendron Trail. Or a cane. Or a broomstick, yardstick, golf club, umbrella or pool cue.

No such luck. It was a rifle.

Angela grabbed my arm and pointed across the road where a katydid was going berserk.

It was Supergranny, of course. I'd been so intrigued by Sore Knees & Rifle that I'd forgotten three katydids followed by an owl hoot meant "regroup."

Angela went first. She lay down and rolled quietly across the road.

I waited a second to see whether Sore Knees noticed.

He didn't, so I sent Shackleford across.

Old Sore Knees didn't budge.

Then I lay down and rolled across. I felt like I made more noise than a freight train, but it must have been my imagination, because when I got to Team One, Sore Knees was still planted on the porch. In fact, he'd leaned against the railing and looked like he was falling asleep.

Supergranny aimed the binoculars at him and grinned.

Then she passed them around. His head was against the railing.

His eyes were open like he was awake, but his mouth hung open like he was asleep.

As I watched, his eyes closed and joined his mouth in sleep.

"Some sentry," Supergranny whispered. "Piece of cake."

"Piece of cake" seemed a little overly optimistic to me.

After all, there *was* a guy with a rifle on the porch.

Plus, the Ferrari meant 6'4" Fake Boots was probably inside with who knew how many ambassador kidnappers.

And here we were, miles from everywhere down a secret road.

On the other hand, we'd been in worse fixes since meeting up with Supergranny. I couldn't think of any right then, but I knew there'd been some.

Piece of cake or not, she wasn't taking chances. "We won't rush it," she whispered. "We'll start with LEBA."

"LEBA" is her code word for "Learn Enemy Before Acting."

In this case we wanted to learn two things:

1. Specific information about Sore Knees. Did he make his lookout rounds of the cabin regularly or at random? For example, did he go every twenty minutes? Every hour? Or when the mood struck?

2. General information about the cabin. Would people be coming and going or were they settled in for the night? Was there another sentry hiding someplace or was Sore Knees a solo? That sort of stuff.

LEBA took a long time.

Sore Knees made his next round in twenty minutes. In between, we could hear voices coming from the cabin, but no one came or left. And there was no sign of another sentry.

Sore Knees circled the cabin twice, stopped to look in the window, then resettled on the top step. Clunk, his head fell against the porch railing.

Supergranny watched through the binoculars and grinned again. She handed them to me. Sore Knees went through his eyes-open-mouth-open-eyes-closed-fast-asleep routine. I nodded to Supergranny and handed her the binoculars.

"Good," she said, taking a quick look. "We'll wait to see if he makes another round in twenty minutes and goes back to sleep. If he does, we'll make our move."

Well, he didn't.

Twenty minutes came and went, and he didn't budge.

The moon climbed directly above the cabin, the voices droned on inside and still Sore Knees snored.

Shackleford and Chesterton, bored and disgusted, crawled under a hemlock tree and went to sleep. Supergranny, Angela, Vannie and I each took ten-minute turns watching Sore Knees while the others sat down to wait.

An hour passed.

"Maybe he's going to sleep all night," I whispered to Supergranny.

"Maybe we should make our move NOW," Vannie whispered. Waiting isn't Vannie's long suit. She hates and despises it.

"Too risky," Supergranny answered. "He might wake up any minute."

At an hour and ten minutes, Angela signaled thumbs up. We all stared through the branches.

Sore Knees stood, stretched, scooped a dipper of drinking water from a pail on the porch, then sipped from the dipper with his right hand and held the rifle with his left as he circled the cabin.

"Some sentry," Supergranny whispered, shaking her head in disapproval. "Pretty sloppy sentry work."

Sloppy he might have been, but his two nice naps and dipper of water seemed to have revived him. He watched through the window for what seemed like years, then did stretching exercises on the porch before finally settling down on the top step.

This time it took him forever to go to sleep. Clunk. At last his head hit the rail. The mouth opened. The eyes closed.

Slowly, Supergranny lowered the binoculars and held up her right hand with fingers outstretched. It meant we moved in five minutes.

Old Sore Knees dozed against the railing.

Five minutes passed.

We broke into Plan 437XKG Phase 2 Teams.

Team One - Supergranny, Vannie and Chesterton circled to the left and to the back of the cabin.

Team Two - Angela, Shackleford and I moved to the right, stopping directly opposite the lighted window.

Angela stayed in the shadows, holding Shackleford while I dashed to the side of the house. I flattened myself against the wall, and gave a quick thumbs-up signal to Angela. I could barely see her signaling back.

As soon as I caught my breath I crouched; then, hugging the side of the house, crept to the window.

I listened beneath the window, and at first could hear nothing. Then muffled voices started again.

I took a deep breath and stood up just high enough to look in the lower right-hand corner of the window.

Fake Boots sat at a table playing solitaire. Two other men sat on cots across the room. Their ankles and one arm each were fastened to the cots with chain. They were talking quietly in a language I couldn't understand.

One of them was small and athletic with receding brown hair and a mustache. "Haji," I said under my breath.

The other was tall, muscular and had bristly red hair and

a beard just like Fake Boots'. "Boots," I said under my breath.

We'd found them! And they only had two guards!

All I had to do was get back to Angela and signal Supergranny and Vannie.

Then Angela, Shackleford and I would watch the cabin while Team One sneaked back to the pickup and summoned the sheriff and FBI.

That's all we had to do.

I'd just turned to do it when screaming, barking, roaring and chaos broke out.

Angela and Shackleford were screaming and barking and racing in circles and something big, dark and furry was roaring as it barreled straight for me.

"HELPPPP! OLD JELLIEEE —" I screamed as he crashed into me and bounced me off the cabin wall.

15

The whole plan was messed up.

Instead of being OUTSIDE the cabin going for the sheriff, FBI and cavalry as planned, we were INSIDE the cabin tied up with Boots and Haji.

"I'm sorry," I kept muttering to Supergranny as Fake Boots tied my ankles to Haji's cot. "It's all my fault."

I'd broken a major rule of Plan 437XKG: SILENCE.

I'd yelled like a maniac the minute Old Jellie bounced me off the cabin. I couldn't seem to help myself. What's more, given the chance, I knew I'd do it again.

Of course, they'd all come running. Supergranny, Angela, Vannie, Chesterton and Shackleford to the rescue and Fake Boots and Sore Knees to catch us. Even tied-up Boots and Haji had dragged their cots to the window to see what the commotion was.

"Don't sweat it, Joshua," Supergranny said as Fake Boots tied her wrists behind her chair, then tied Shackleford to the table leg beside her. "It's only human to yell when a bear bounces you off a cabin."

"Especially if it's a surprise," Real Boots said.

"I'd have yelled, too, Josh," Vannie put in.

"Me too, Jush," Haji said. He pronounced "Josh" as "Jush."

We'd all introduced ourselves, sort of, while Fake Boots and Sore Knees were dragging and pushing and shoving us into the cabin with the help of the butt of Sore Knees' rifle.

"I DID yell," Angela reminded me. "And Shackleford barked her head off."

Poor Shackleford stuck her head under Supergranny's chair in embarrassment.

The only one who'd gotten away was Old Jellie. Apparently, he hadn't meant us any harm. He'd just blundered into our little operation by mistake, wreaked havoc and mayhem, then vanished into the woods.

It was just as well. It was crowded enough in there without a blundering black bear.

Fake Boots was in a snit.

He was no more thrilled and delighted to have us than we were thrilled and delighted to be there.

"HOW DID YOU FIND US? HOW?" he demanded.

"HOWHOWHOWHOWHOW?" Sore Knees echoed shrilly, waving his rifle and jumping around like a stiff-legged elf.

"ANSWER ME!" Fake Boots thundered.

"ANSWER HIM, TURKEYS. ANSWER HIM, *NOW*. RIGHT *NOW*!!" Sore Knees chattered. He seemed glad to be in the cabin after the long, dull hours on the porch. He seemed bored, dumb and dangerous.

"SHUT UP, LEROY!" Fake Boots yelled, then turned back to us. "IS ANYBODY ELSE OUT THERE?"

"ANYBODY OUT THERE? WHO'S OUT THERE? WHO'S WHERE OUT THERE?" Sore Knees Leroy shrilled, jumping up and down and landing on Fake Boots' foot.

Fake Boots exploded. "OUT," he screamed. "LEROY, GET OUT OF HERE."

Leroy's grin faded. He looked hurt.

"Gee, keep your pants on," he said. "I'm just trying to help. A person tries to help around here and everybody blows up at him just for doing his job. Gee, a person tries to help and — "

"Porch, Leroy," Fake Boots hissed through clenched teeth. "PORCHPORCHPORCHPORCHPORCH!"

Leroy went to the porch.

Supergranny, Boots and Haji took advantage of the fuss to whisper quietly in a strange language I figured must be Balkhastani.

"QUIET," Fake Boots snarled, spinning around.

He grilled us for about an hour.

Supergranny did most of the talking — slipping at once into her basic Dithery Old Lady act. She rehearses it faithfully once a month at home to keep in top form.

She pretended not to hear about every third question Fake Boots asked and to misunderstand any question she didn't want to answer. Then she dragged out answers to the questions she didn't mind answering and wandered from the subject whenever she thought she could get away with it.

Of course, she had to be careful not to overdo it, because Fake Boots had already seen her in action. Besides, he knew she drove a Ferrari and might get suspicious if she overdid the dithery. So she did a toned-down dithery.

Supergranny doing a Dithery Old Lady act signals us to slip into our Innocent Young Kids act.

She insists we rehearse our Innocent Young Kids act with her once a month whether we need to or not.

"It's a good defense," she always says, "but it takes practice."

In this case doing an Innocent Young Kids act just meant we acted sleepy, pretended to forget stuff we didn't want to answer and backed up what Supergranny told Fake Boots.

And what did she tell him?

— That we'd seen the limousine go into the woods the day before and were curious.

— That we'd been surprised to see the Ferrari outside and came up to investigate.

That's about all Fake Boots was able to pry out of her in an hour.

She didn't tell him zip about the "He's Not Boots" coded message.

I don't think he even realized we knew Haji was Haji.

Finally, Fake Boots seemed worn down.

He tried one last question: "Who are you working for?"

She started out saying she'd worked for a law firm until '57, but in recent years worked at home, where she did enjoy cooking, especially baking.

Next thing we knew she was giving him her snicker-doodle recipe (leaving out the crucial ingredient).

It was a masterful performance.

Fake Boots groaned, gave up, and stared out the window where night had turned to pale gray dawn. Suddenly tires crunched on the gravel outside the cabin. Car doors slammed.

Wonderful images of sheriffs, police, and FBI agents flashed through my brain.

No such luck. Whoever it was, Fake Boots was glad to see them.

He glanced at his watch and smiled.

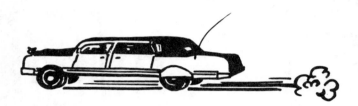

16

The limo was back.

We could see it and at least one Ford through the open cabin door.

The door was open because Leroy had just burst in with four guys wearing baggy purple pants, blue earrings, and scarves tied around their heads.

That's right — baggy purple pants, blue earrings, and scarves tied around their heads.

"They look like escapees from Ali Baba and the Forty Thieves," Angela muttered.

"Or Treasure Island," Vannie muttered.

"Or Balkhastan," Haji muttered. "Note the beautiful lapis lazuli earrings. Pure Balkhastani lapis lazuli, no doubt about it."

We could mutter because the crooks were ignoring us

while they shouted at each other in Balkhastani — except for Leroy, who just laughed hysterically and did stiff-legged jumps around the room.

"They're planning to leave and take Boots and me with them," Haji translated. "But they can't decide how to ride — everybody wants to ride in the limo, and nobody wants to ride in the Ford."

The din was horrible, but we were grateful to have the spotlight off us for a minute.

"They're leaving you here with Leroy," Haji said.

At that, Boots leaned toward me and dropped something in my hand. "When you get away, give this to your mom," he whispered quickly, "and give her and your dad my love. And thanks for trying to help."

Just then, the crooks finally stopped shouting and started untying Boots and Haji and herding them outside.

"*Montani Semper Liberi,*" Boots said to us with a grin and a quick thumbs-up as he and Haji were pushed through the door. It was Latin for "Mountaineers are Always Free."

Under cover of the uproar, Supergranny whispered something to Angela. Angela whispered something to Vannie. Vannie glanced at me, and pretended to sneeze, covering the side of her mouth with her hand. "732T," she whispered. "As soon as they leave."

I stared at her.

Surely, I hadn't heard right.

Or had Supergranny gone bonkers?

Plan 732T meant Dive Out the Back Window and Head for the Hills in 74 Seconds or Less.

81

With Supergranny, Angela and Vannie tied to chairs?
Shackleford and Chesterton tied to a table leg?
Me tied to a cot?
Great. Wonderful. Terrific.
I couldn't wait to see how we did it.

*   *   *   *   *   *

Real Boots, Haji, Fake Boots, Leroy, and the Baggy Pants Quartet moved outside amid much bumping, threatening, yelling and confusion.

The door closed.

Instantly, Supergranny pulled the Swiss army knife she carries everywhere out of her left stars-and-stripes tennis shoes.

"Thanks, Shackleford," she whispered, in one smooth motion slicing the rope tying Shackleford and Chesterton to the table.

Her hands had been free almost the whole time! Shackleford had only PRETENDED to crawl under the chair out of embarrassment. She'd really been under there chewing through the rope around Supergranny's wrists!

A car door slammed. Uh-oh. They were getting loaded. Any minute the limo and Ford would take off and Leroy would pop back in to play Guard the Prisoners.

Supergranny sliced the rope from Angela's hands and feet, and handed her the knife.

Another car door slammed. Then another. Slam, slam, slam, slam, slam, slam.

Under cover of the door slams, Supergranny unhooked

and unhinged the back window screen and tossed it outside.

Meanwhile, Angela cut at the rope from Vannie's wrists, and Shackleford gnawed at the rope tying my ankles to the cot.

An engine started.

Supergranny grabbed Chesterton and tossed him out the window.

"Hurry," she hissed at Angela.

"My fingers are numb," Angela hissed back. She finally cut the rope from Vannie's wrists and started on her ankle ropes.

Shackleford gnawed at the rope tying my ankles to the cot.

"Hurry, Shackleford," I whispered.

The limousine and Ford were pulling away.

Angela got the rope off Vannie's ankles.

"Out," Supergranny hissed at Vannie, boosting her out the window. "To the trees. Follow Chesterton."

We could hear Leroy thumping toward the door.

Shackleford kept gnawing at my ankle ropes, while Angela sawed back and forth on my wrist rope.

"Forget his hands, just cut him loose from the cot," Supergranny hissed.

Leroy lifted the door latch.

Angela pushed Shackleford out of the way and started cutting at Shackleford's gnawing spot. Shackleford hurdled through the window after Vannie.

The knife sliced through the rope. I was free!

My hands still tied behind me, Supergranny pushed me out the window. I landed in a somersault, rolled and just kept rolling, as fast as I could roll, after Shackleford.

Angela jumped through the window with Supergranny on her heels as Leroy burst into the room. They scooped me up by the armpits, one on each side, and dragged me into the woods.

Out the window came Leroy, firing his rifle wildly and bellowing like a baby.

He couldn't run very fast because of his sore knees. Thank heavens for that because we were running almost straight up a rocky hill through dense underbrush. And me with my hands behind my back!

Up we scrambled in the shadowy dawn.

Supposed we did lose Leroy? Would we lose ourselves, too? Would we ever find our way out of some of the ruggedest country in America?

My lungs felt ready to burst and my heart seemed to pound in my ears. Or *was* it my heart?

"It's the falls," Supergranny gasped. "Follow the sound. Full speed ahead to Devil Creek Falls."

17

We collapsed in heaps on the bridge at Devil Creek Falls.

I just lay on my stomach with one cheek pressed into the bridge planks and my eyes staring at the swirling water below.

Somebody — I didn't know or care if it was Super-granny, Angela or the governor of West Virginia — cut the rope from my wrists and told me to wiggle my fingers.

Where was Leroy?

I didn't care about that, either. If he could make it up that hill with his knees, he was welcome to us.

My own knees felt like dried-out sponges, my lungs and nose had forgotten how to breathe together, my ankles were raw with pain and my arms and cheeks stung with a thousand bramble scratches.

My only goals in life were:

(1) Keep lying on the bridge.

(2) Retrain my nose and lungs to breathe together.

In that order.

It was not to be.

"UP!" Supergranny shouted. "UPUPUP!"

"TO THE LODGE. WE'VE GOT TO GET TO THE LODGE AND STOP THAT LIMO."

Don't ask me how she planned to stop the limo at the lodge. Maybe by calling the police, I don't know.

But it was the lodge or bust.

Before I could gasp, "Go on without me," she and Angela had me by the armpits again, lugging me to my feet.

"Annie Scott Woods' shortcut to the Rhododendron Trail," Supergranny barked. "Double pronto."

Chesterton led. Once his memory is programmed with a shortcut, it's there for eternity. We didn't miss a turn.

Onward and upward we staggered, arriving at the lodge with the morning sun.

*   *   *   *   *   *

Trivia question:

How long does it take to jump out the window of Fake Boots' hideout, scramble up the mountain to Devil Creek Falls, cross to the Rhododendron Trail and climb to the Devil Mountain Lodge while being chased by a wild man firing a rifle?

Answer:

EXACTLY as long as it takes a gang of crooks to drive a limo and Ford down the hideout's dirt lane to the paved road, then wind around the highway to the Devil Mountain Lodge.

$$* \qquad * \qquad * \qquad * \qquad * \qquad *$$

The instant we crested the hill to the Devil Mountain Lodge parking lot, we saw two things.

First, the limo and Ford whipped past on the mountain highway.

Second, the senior citizens' bus parked outside the lodge's main entrance with its motor rumbling, warming up for the trip to Nashville. Everybody was on board except Frank, who was loading baggage, and Annie Scott Woods, who was supervising.

"FORGET THOSE BAGS, WE'VE GOT AN EMERGENCY," Supergranny roared, swooping across the parking lot.

Before you could say *"Montani Semper Liberi,"* she had Frank in the driver's seat and herself and Annie Scott Woods hovering over him, clinging to the dash.

Chesterton, Angela and Vannie clambered up the bus steps past them.

"FOLLOW THAT LIMO!" Supergranny yelled, as I pushed up the steps, dragging a suddenly bashful Shackleford behind me.

Frank closed the doors and drove across the parking lot. Slowly. Agonizingly slowly. He looked puzzled, worried and scared.

"MOVE IT!" Supergranny thundered.

"Now just a cotton pickin' minute, Mrs. Oglepop," Frank protested, slowly shifting gears. Agonizingly slowly. "I can't just —"

Exasperated, Supergranny turned to Annie Scott Woods. "DO something with your grandson, Annie. We've GOT to catch the limo. It's a national emergency. I'll explain later."

"Move it, Frank," Annie said in her throaty voice.

"Grandma, I can't just —"

"If Sadie says it's a national emergency, it's a national emergency," Annie said. "Do it for your country, Frank."

That did it.

Frank slammed the gearshaft into third. The bus lurched forward and peeled out of the parking lot onto the narrow, two-lane highway.

We were off!

Supergranny and Annie hovered by the windshield advising Frank while the rest of us worked the aisles, informing the troops.

In other words, we had to explain to sixty-one senior citizens why their tour bus was careening down a twisty mountain after a limousine.

Luckily, most of them had read that Ambassador Haji Jamad was missing, a few of them had seen the strange limo whip past, and all of them liked a little excitement.

So it wasn't very hard convincing them this crazy chase made sense.

The hard part was to make them stop laughing while we convinced them.

They were laughing because Vannie, Angela and I were

having a hideous time standing up in the aisle. Once Frank decided to take off, he really TOOK OFF, rounding curves so fast that Angela, Vannie and I bounced around the aisle like vollyballs.

The senior citizens kept grabbing us to keep us from falling. Every time they caught us they laughed in relief and every time they missed us they laughed harder.

Meanwhile, we weren't just lurching from side to side around curves.

Oh no. If you think that, you don't know West Virginia.

We were lurching from side to side around curves WHILE GOING UP AND DOWN STEEP HILLS. And every time we went DOWNHILL, Shackleford and Chesterton slid clear to the front of the bus, knocking us down en route if we weren't quick enough to jump over them.

And every time we went UPHILL, here rolled Shackleford and Chesterton back again, bowling-ball style.

It must have been some show because I'd never seen a busload of senior citizens laugh so hard in my life and, with luck, I never will again.

Finally they stopped laughing and began to cheer. An elderly couple pulled me into their seat so I could see what the cheering was about.

I squashed my nose against their window and looked straight down.

We were at the top of the hairpin curve so steep all I could see for hundreds of feet was air.

And way down at the bottom of the air was the rest of the hairpin turn. And on it sped a skidding limousine and a tailgating Ford.

89

"FASTER, FRANK!" the elderly man beside me yelled.

"FASTER, FRANK!" yelled his death-defying wife.

The other senior citizens took up the chant. "Faster, Frank! Faster, Frank! Faster, Frank."

The rear end of the bus skidded as we rounded the steep curve. All I could see out the window was steep mountain dropoffs of air. I closed my eyes.

The bus straightened out and shot smack down the middle of the road.

"FASTER, FRANK!" chanted the senior citizens.

"Don't let anything come the other way," I prayed under my breath. "Please don't let anything come the other way."

We rounded another curve just in time for the people in the front of the bus to see the tail of the Ford rounding the curve ahead.

"We're gaining on 'em!" the people in the front shouted over their shoulders to the people in the middle of the bus.

"Gaining on 'em!" the people in the middle shouted over their shoulders to the people in the back.

"Gating 'em!" the people in the back yelled. Everybody cheered.

We rounded one more curve.

The people in the front saw it first.

They screamed.

The rest of us leaned in the aisle for a better view.

We screamed.

Road construction dead ahead. Man in hard hat waving stop sign on pole. Limo, Ford, and bus heading straight for dump truck crossing road. Steep mountain wall on right. Steep mountain dropoff on left. Frank hits brakes. Brakes scream in ears. Mountain wall whips past.

Limo sliding toward dump truck. Man in hardhat jumping off mountain. Stop sign on pole flying through air. Ford sliding sideways toward thousand-foot drop.

Bus barrels straight on, brakes scream, rear end fishtails.

Bus bumps to a halt.

No crash.

"AFTER THEM!" Supergranny shouted. Frank jammed the door lever open, and Supergranny and Annie leaped off the bus, followed by Frank, Angela, Vannie, Chesterton, Shackleford and me, followed by sixty-one enraged senior citizens.

Fake Boots, Real Boots, Haji and a purple, baggy-pants duet sprang from the limo. It had crashed into the dump truck and had a stop sign lodged in its windshield.

Another purple, baggy-pants duet climbed ever so gingerly from the Ford, which had two rear wheels hanging over the thousand-foot drop.

Supergranny leaped for Fake Boots and downed him with a flying tackle. Shackleford, forgetting to be shy, bounced after them.

"SIT," I yelled, which Shackleford did — right square in the middle of Fake Boots' back.

Fake Boots tried to push Shackleford and Supergranny off him, but it was hopeless because Chesterton had already clamped onto his left hand and was holding on. And Annie had already bit into his right hand and was holding on.

So much for Fake Boots!

Meanwhile, Frank got mixed up and was chasing Haji, who was chasing the first baggy-pants duet.

"NO, FRANK, HE'S THE GOOD GUY!" Angela yelled.

"THE LITTLE GUY'S THE GOOD GUY," Vannie yelled.

Just in time, Frank got the message. Instead of grabbing Haji, he grabbed a baggy-pants. Haji grabbed the other one.

They were down!

Back at the Ford, the other two baggy-pants were surrounded by sixty-one enraged senior citizens.

"How dare you try to kidnap an ambassador visiting our country?" scolded the woman who had shared her seat with me.

"How dare you try it in our beautiful West Virginia?" scolded her husband.

Angela and Vannie helped Boots sit down and lean against the limo as they patted blood from his face with handkerchiefs.

"It's just my arm," Boots said. "Just a little cut from when the stop sign broke the window."

"It's just his arm," Angela echoed. "He just got a little blood on his face from a small cut on his arm."

Supergranny finished tying Fake Boots' ankles and wrists together with the special grosgrain ribbon she carries everywhere. Then she tossed the ribbon spool to Haji to truss up the baggy-pants gang.

"Stay," she ordered Shackleford. Shackleford barked proudly and stayed — still as a statue planted in the small of Fake Boots' back.

Just then, a hand appeared over the roadside retaining wall.

I grabbed it and helped the construction worker over the wall from the grassy ledge he'd landed on when he leaped out of sight.

"WHAT in the *@@##*! is going on?" he asked. "And where's my stop sign?"

"There, there, I can explain everything," Supergranny said, patting his arm. "It's all over but the explanation."

"And the celebration," Boots said with a grin. "This calls for a celebration."

Supergranny laughed and bowed to the sixty-one senior citizens, Annie Scott Woods and Frank.

"Boots is right. This calls for a party to celebrate. At my workshop-office-laboratory-playroom-garage. You're all invited. Can you all make it to my place in Illinois?"

Sixty-one senior citizens, Annie Scott Woods and Frank cheered. Of course they could make it. Was she kidding? Mention "party" to this group and they'd make it to the moon.

It was quite a party.

Mom and Dad got back from Spain the night before. Frank, Annie Scott Woods and the sixty-one senior citizens came on their bus and took over a whole floor of the Sheraton Hotel downtown.

Boots and Haji flew in from Washington, where they'd been meeting with the Justice Department about Fake Boots & Gang.

Supergranny, Angela, Vannie and I spent the whole day in her kitchen baking snickerdoodles. Don't ask how many because I lost count after twelve dozen.

We finished just in time to go home and change, then race back before the party started at 7 p.m. Supergranny wanted us IN her workshop-office-laboratory-playroom-garage before the guests arrived.

"We'll have the guests use the garage door," she said. "I'd rather keep quiet about the fireplace doors for security reasons."

Of course Supergranny, Angela, Vannie, Shackleford and I used the fireplace doors.

At the last minute we loaded what seemed about ten million snickerdoodles onto Supergranny's tea cart and lined up in front of the hearth in the kitchen.

Each of us munched a snickerdoodle made by the special secret recipe.

"Shackleford, it's your turn to do the honors," Supergranny said.

Shackleford sniffed around for the yellow button just inside the hearth and nudged it with her round, rubbery black nose.

Instantly the fireplace divided in the middle and opened like sliding doors, and "Stars and Stripes Forever" boomed from the ceiling.

Supergranny pushed the tea cart into her office and we all jumped in after her as the fireplace doors clamped shut behind us.

We just made it.

All 67 guests, including Mom and Dad, were thundering up the driveway, and Chesterton was going berserk thinking he'd have to greet them and start the party by himself.

"Joshua, now it's your turn to do the honors," Supergranny said to me.

I pushed the garage door opener, and the guests swarmed inside.

As I said before, it was quite a party!

Annie Scott Woods made a beeline for the southeast corner.

Some people think the southeast corner is the most interesting part of Supergranny's office. It's separated from the rest of the room by a white picket fence with a gate. Directions are posted on the fence:

1. Lock the gate.
2. Push the button beside the activity you want.

There's a long list of activities with buttons beside them mounted along one side of the fence. "Basketball Court," "Swimming Pool," "Helicopter Pad" and "Costume Room," for example.

Annie locked the gate and pushed "Costume Room." A yellow and white striped curtain fell, and before you could say *"Montani Semper Liberi"* it rose again.

And there was a humongous closet lined with rows of costumes. Musketeer outfits complete with plumed hats, swords and mustaches; House of Lords robes with powdered wigs; Michael Jackson outfits, each with a sequined glove. In short, the works.

Before you knew it, everybody was sashaying around in costumes, singing and dancing and eating snickerdoodles and hitting the vending machines.

Supergranny's office has a vending machine balcony with about anything you want in the way of food. Anything you want in the way of anything, in fact — markers (just push the color you want), paperback books, hardback books, videos — all there at the push of a button. No money required.

Mom and Boots couldn't tear themselves away from the caviar/liverwurst/cream-cheese-on-crackers machine.

And Haji and Dad went goofy over the pickled — yuck — herring.

"Delightful room, Sadie, just delightful," Annie Scott Woods said, knocking her Queen Isabella crown cockeyed as she hugged Supergranny. She'd picked the Spanish queen's costume from the costume room in honor of Mom and Dad's trip.

After we'd shot pool, swam, played tennis, volleyball and bingo, bowled, danced, played Pictionary, poker, pitch and pinochle, sang the Balkhastani national anthem thirty-two times, sang the "Star-Spangled Banner" thirty-two times, sang about the Green and White of Marshall University 104 times, and popped 732 helium balloons, we settled down in Supergranny's conversation pit to rehash the crime.

And I gave Mom the pin.

Remember when Boots left us with Sore Knees Leroy at the cabin he'd dropped something in my hand?

"When you get away, give this to your mom," he'd whispered. "And give her and your dad my love."

Luckily, things had turned out ten thousand times better then it appeared they would at the time, and Boots was sitting right there when I gave her the pin he'd dropped in my hand.

She laughed, fastened it to her collar and hugged Boots.

"Whoa, hang on," Angela said, peering at it. "That's a boot pin just like mine." She showed Mom the tiny boot pinned to her pocket.

"Mine's the one we found pinned to the coded message in the garbage that morning," she added.

"Yeah," Vannie said. "How DID that message and pin

97

get in our garbage, anyway?"

"I sent it," Boots said quietly. "By courier."

"Cory what?" Vannie asked.

"Courier," Boots repeated. "It means someone who carries messages."

"But who?" Angela asked.

Boots smiled. "I'll give you three clues. He's furry, he's strong, and his initials are O.J."

"Old Jellie?" I asked. "Old Jellie is a courier bear?"

"The best courier bear in West Virginia," Boots answered. "I've used him for years."

"Maybe you'd better begin at the beginning, Boots," Supergranny suggested. "Tell us how Fake Boots got into the act, who was doing the shooting, everything."

Boots leaned back with his hands behind his head, cracked his knuckles and stretched out his long legs.

"It's a long story," he said slowly.

"Then do a three-in-one," Annie Scott Woods said quickly. "Because I want to hear it, and I'm too tired for a long story. I want to go back to the Sheraton and hit the sack."

She had a point. About a third of the senior citizens were already dozing and I was bushed myself.

Angela explained three-in-one rules to Boots. "You have to tell it in three sentences. In one minute," she said.

Boots said he'd give it a try. Supergranny tossed me her stopwatch, and I started the countdown.

"Ten, nine, eight, seven, six, five, four, three, two, one, go!" I said.

He was off:

"A bunch of thugs planned to overthrow the Balkhastani democracy by capturing Haji and using him as a figurehead king, and one of the thugs had plastic surgery so he'd look like me, poor guy, and practiced for months to act like me so the ordinary folks in Balkhastan would believe Haji and I were a team like in the old days and were running the country, but Haji got wind of it and cabled me to meet him secretly while he was at the Greenbrier Hotel in West Virginia at a meeting with the U.S. Undersecretary of State."

"Twenty seconds," I said.

"Meanwhile," he went on, "the thugs caught on that he'd caught on, flew to the States and tried to scare me off with wild shots at my pickup and threatening phone calls and when that didn't work, they stormed the cabin, threw me in a Ford, and set up a roadblock to stop Haji's limousine, which was easy because, unknown to Haji, his driver was in on the plot."

"Forty seconds," I said.

"So they took us to a little cabin they'd rented from Leroy to hide out until the heat was off, then the plan was to drive us to a secret airfield and fly us back to Balkhastan after sending Fake Boots to fool Supergranny and even staging a fake shooting at him, but Supergranny and troops got wise to Fake Boots, found us, broke up the plot, and caught the limousine and Ford on the way to the airfield, thus saving my hide and Balkhastani democracy!"

100

"TIME" I yelled, waking up the senior citizens, who broke into another chorus of the Balkhastani national anthem followed by the "Star-Spangled Banner."

After we'd stopped the limo, Supergranny had directed the police to Leroy's cabin. They'd found him hiding in the outhouse and the Ferrari, safe but totally dirty, still parked outside.

So the complete Fake Boots Gang was now behind bars, including the drivers of all the other Fords who'd been caught waiting at the secret airfield.

"Great three-in-one, Boots," Vannie said. "Except you still didn't tell about Old Jellie."

"Oops, sorry," Boots said. "Do I get another minute, Annie?" he asked.

"If you make it snappy, dear," Annie said with a yawn.

"Well, there's not much to tell except Haji and I trained Old Jellie to take messages to my house when we were home from Harvard during college breaks.

"When the crooks had us tied up in Leroy's cabin, Old Jellie kept hanging around, and the night you got in I was able to slip him the message through the window.

"I wanted to warn you that Fake Boots wasn't me, so I wrote 'He's not Boots' in the code your Mom and I used when we were kids, hoping that you'd get it. And I used one of the boot pins I'm always giving people, hoping you'd know it was really me."

"Speaking of the code, something still puzzles me," Angela said. "What's COBBLERU NDERCOUCH?"

Boots looked blank.

"Say, what?" he asked.

"COBBLERU NDERCOUCH?" Angela repeated, pulling the paper she'd found in the "Five Little Peppers Book" from her pocket.

She handed it to Boots, who showed it to Mom.

"It's how we cracked your code, but we never understood the message," Angela said.

Boots and Mom began to laugh. Then they laughed harder. Then they laughed so hard they gasped for breath and we had to pound them both on the back.

"It means: Cobbler —" Boots gasped.

"— Under Couch," Mom finished.

"My mother had baked a blackberry cobbler," Boots explained, wiping tears from his eyes. "But our Bowen cousins were coming to visit and we knew once they lit into it there wouldn't be any left for supper . . . so I hid it under the couch."

"And he left me the note," Mom picked up. "In code '— Cobbler Under Couch.' "

Everybody laughed so hard they got their second wind, and next thing you knew, Mom and Boots were playing a harmonica duet of "Turkey in the Straw" over and over because it was the only song they knew.

And Haji invited us all to visit Balkhastan, while Chesterton climbed into Supergranny's lap and switched off his lights and beeper, and Annie scratched Shackleford behind the ear and forgot about hitting the sack at the Sheraton.

And pictures of Spain and Balkhastan and West Virginia swirled through my head. And lapis lazuli, limousines and Haji saying, "Me, too, Jush." And cabins tucked deep in hazy mountains.

Around and around it all danced in my head.

And Mom and Boots played another round of "Turkey in the Straw" . . . and I didn't mind. I didn't mind at all.

ABOUT THE AUTHOR

Beverly Van Hook grew up in Huntington, West Virginia, and now lives in Rock Island, Illinois. She is an award-winning journalist who has written numerous articles for national magazines. She is married to an advertising executive and has three children and an Old English sheepdog exactly like Shackleford.

ABOUT THE ARTIST

Catherine Wayson grew up in Iowa and now lives in Huntsville, Alabama, where she is a full-time professional illustrator and free-lance artist and photographer. Her paintings and photographs have appeared in juried shows nationally and throughout the Midwest.